If ~~*...... ....*~~ *sense she'd ask him to leave right now.*

The tilt of his chin and the smoky look in his eyes gave him away. He was going to say something that would have sounded like heaven ten years ago. "Rumor has it you only have peanut butter in the house for dinner. How 'bout steak and fries at the coffee shop? I'm buying," he said.

"I don't think that's a good idea."

"You're on a diet of peanut butter and junk food?"

"Hawk, we gave everyone in town plenty to talk about ten years ago. I'm not interested in going through that again. Besides, you'll ruin your reputation hanging around with me," she warned.

"I'm willing to risk it."

Dear Reader,

This month we have a wonderful lineup of books for you—romantic reading that's sure to take the chill out of these cool winter nights.

What happens when two precocious kids advertise for a new father—and a new husband—for their mom? The answer to that question and *much* more can be found in the delightful *Help Wanted: Daddy* by Carolyn Monroe. This next book in our FABULOUS FATHERS series is filled with love, laughter and larger-than-life hero Boone Shelton—a truly irresistible candidate for fatherhood.

We're also very pleased to present Diana Palmer's latest Romance, *King's Ransom*. A spirited heroine and a royal hero marry first and find love later in this exciting and passionate story. We know you won't want to miss it.

Don't forget to visit that charming midwestern town, Duncan, Oklahoma, in *A Wife Worth Waiting For*, the conclusion to Arlene James's THIS SIDE OF HEAVEN trilogy. Bolton Charles, who has appeared in earlier titles, finally meets his match in Clarice Revere. But can Bolton convince her that he's unlike the domineering men in her past?

Rounding out the list, Joan Smith's *Poor Little Rich Girl* is a breezy, romantic treat. And Kari Sutherland makes a welcome return with *Heartfire, Homefire*. We are also proud to present the debut of a brand-new author in Romance, Charlotte Moore with *Not the Marrying Kind*. When the notorious Beth Haggerty returns to her hometown, she succeeds in stirring up just as much gossip as always—and just as much longing in the heart of Deputy Sheriff Raymond Hawk.

In the months ahead, there are more wonderful romances coming your way by authors such as Annette Broadrick, Elizabeth August, Marie Ferrarella, Carla Cassidy and many more. Please write to us with your comments and suggestions. We take your opinions to heart.

Happy reading,

Anne Canadeo
Senior Editor

NOT THE MARRYING KIND
Charlotte Moore

Silhouette
R O M A N C E™
Published by Silhouette Books
America's Publisher of Contemporary Romance

This one is for the Lunch Bunch, who have faithfully
rooted for me even when they didn't quite know
what I was up to. My deepest thanks for your
enduring friendship.

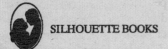 SILHOUETTE BOOKS

ISBN 0-373-08975-9

NOT THE MARRYING KIND

Printed in U.S.A.

CHARLOTTE MOORE

has always enjoyed putting words on paper. Until recently, most of these words have been nonfiction, including a weekly newspaper column that has recruited nearly twenty thousand volunteers in the past twenty years for some four hundred different local nonprofit organizations.

When she is not urging people to get involved in their community, Charlotte divides her time among writing, volunteering for her favorite organizations (including Orange County Chapter of Romance Writers of America), trying *not* to mother two married daughters and sharing her life in Southern California with her own special hero, Chuck.

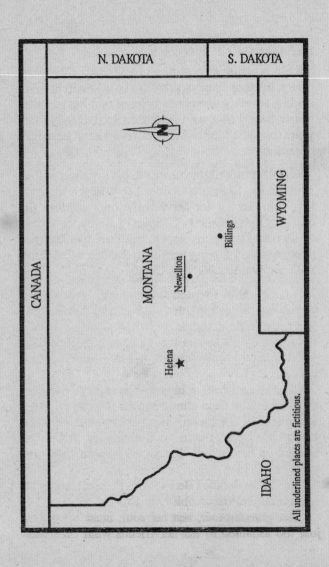

All underlined places are fictitious.

Chapter One

"Did you know Beth Haggerty is back in town?"

Very slowly Hawk lowered his booted feet from the edge of the desk, swiveled his chair and listened with heightened interest to the caller on the phone. "I hadn't heard that, Myrtle."

"Just blew into town this afternoon. Mercy, that girl is nothing but trouble. Always has been. Just like her sister."

If Hawk had been a big-city cop, Myrtle Symington would have been considered an informant. Here in Newellton, Montana, her grocery store was the center of much of the town's activity, and Hawk depended on her to keep him up-to-date on the latest news.

Smiling, he doodled Beth's name on a yellow pad of paper while Myrtle rambled on nonstop.

"Her grandmother, rest her soul, must have been just too ashamed to tell her friends what that little rascal really does for a living in New York. Do you know what she is? *Really?*"

A mischievous teenager who'd grown into a strikingly beautiful young woman, based on the quick glimpse he'd had of Beth a couple of months ago when she'd come to town to bury her grandmother.

"What's that, Myrtle?"

"She's a...*stripper.*" The last word came out in a secretive whisper.

Hawk's pencil point snapped. "I'd heard—" He cleared the laugh that tickled his throat.

"Oh, I'd heard different, too. But that's what she told me, plain as day, her standing right here at my checkout counter buying nothing but junk food and peanut butter."

"I see." Given Myrtle's very active imagination, it was darn hard to sort through the chaff to get the kernel.

"You'd better look into this, Hawk. We don't want that young lady starting any strip shows here in Newellton. We're not that kind of town."

"I'll be happy to check on things, Myrtle." He was more than pleased to have an excuse to see Beth Haggerty again.

He cradled the phone and was still enjoying the play of memories through his mind when it rang again.

"Sheriff's office. Hawk speaking."

"Isn't there a law agin' settin' up massage parlors in this town?" he heard Jake Martins ask, the sounds of his busy garage in the background.

Hawk gave his phone a puzzled look. "I guess I don't know the answer to that right off. How come you're asking?"

"It's Beth Haggerty. She's back in town and..."

A massage parlor? Hawk nearly choked. Beth was certainly making her presence known.

Three phone calls later, Hawk lifted his hat from the coatrack in the corner of his cubicle-size office and placed it squarely on his head. A smile tugged at the corners of his mouth.

Watch out, Newellton. Beth Haggerty is back in town.

"Hawk!" She expelled his name in a breathless whisper. "I didn't expect— What are you doing..." And why was she standing at the screen door of her grandmother's house experiencing a dizzying sensation of déjà vu?

"I heard you were back in town, Beth. I thought I'd drop by to see how you were getting along."

Her gaze slid from his incredibly dark eyes and classically sculpted cheekbones to the unexpected badge pinned on his uniformed chest and the holstered gun at his hip. "You're a sheriff?"

"Deputy." His lips canted into a cocky grin, familiar and breathtakingly masculine. "Wouldn't want my boss to think I'm trying to take over his job."

"Of course not. I'm just surprised...." She felt as if her mouth was filled with a whole bag of cotton balls, while her heart beat crazily against her ribs. "Come on in."

She shoved open the screen door to admit the man she hadn't seen in ten years, the first man—not boy—who had ever kissed her. If at fifteen she'd thought of Hawk as daunting, it was only because she'd never envisioned him as he was today—lean, hard, with legs that went on forever and eyes that appraised her with blatant masculine approval. The ribbed tank top she'd changed into after her flight from New York gave her very little protection from Hawk's thorough scrutiny. She resisted the urge to fold her arms across her chest in self-defense.

"I'm afraid the house is a mess," she said, pulling a white dust cover off an overstuffed couch. "I couldn't stay around after Grandmother's funeral so I just closed up the house as best I could, planning to come back when I got the time."

"No problem." He stood in the middle of the living room, his stance comfortable with feet spread wide apart, while he slowly shifted his Smoky-the-Bear sheriff's hat in his hands. Without even trying, he managed to dwarf everything in the room, Beth Haggerty included.

She swallowed uncomfortably. "I can't even offer you a cup of coffee. It'll be a day or two before I can get the gas turned back on for the stove. There's electricity, though. Would you like something cold to drink?"

"Only if it's easy."

Easy. That's what Hawk and everyone else had thought of Beth before she'd left the "Gossip Capital of the World." As nearly as she could tell, Newellton's city fathers included a whole lot of prairie dogs in their population count that claimed five thousand.

"At least the refrigerator is working," she said, pushing through the swinging door to the kitchen, acutely aware of how closely Hawk walked behind her. If she hesitated and turned, she'd be in his arms in a second...and she hadn't thought about that for years. She shouldn't be considering the idea now.

She pulled open the refrigerator and retrieved two cans from the bottom shelf. "It's only diet cola." She offered one to Hawk. "You want a glass or—"

"The can's fine."

With a quick flick of his wrist, he popped the tab, then settled one lean hip on the edge of the maple kitchen table. "So how long do you plan to be in town?"

"Couple of weeks. I need to get the house winterized and ready to sell. Or maybe rent, if I have to. I can't exactly afford to keep up the taxes and maintenance on the place."

He took a long swig from the can. Against her will, Beth found herself strangely fascinated by the masculine movement of his Adam's apple. In spite of his dark hair, long and tied back with a thong, and his burnished complexion, there was almost no sign of a five-o'clock shadow, though it was already late afternoon. His smooth skin was typical of the Crow Indians in the region, and very appealing. Even after all these years she could still recall the feel of her hand palming his cheek, a wayward thought that shot a flush up her neck.

"You figure your clients can get along without you for a while?" he asked, studying her over the top of the can.

"Forget the clients. I was way overdue for a vacation." She leaned back against the tile counter near the sink, making a conscious effort to keep Hawk at a distance. "I had a couple of horrendous deadlines to meet—illustrating a commercial for a new brand of jeans and then another account for an absorbs-all paper towel—or I would have stayed around after Grandma Claire died. I've been working twenty-hour days for longer than I care to remember. But everything's under control at the moment." Except for the dark circles she'd noticed under her eyes and a general malaise that was probably endemic to the advertising industry.

The corners of his eyes crinkled and he swiped the back of his hand across his mouth, as though he was making a real effort not to smile. "Funny, I wasn't aware strippers led such pressure-filled lives."

Beth choked on her cola. "Stripper? My God, you've heard that rumor already?" She'd only dropped that little bombshell two hours ago.

"I've had a couple of calls this afternoon," he admitted dryly. "Can't imagine where folks get such crazy ideas."

"You know Myrtle Symington—Gossip Queen of Newellton."

"Even she needs a little help to create a tale like that." He shoved away from the table. In two strides he was standing next to Beth, his khaki shirt and the way it outlined his broad chest filling her view. "May I assume you had something to do with the latest rumor?"

With difficulty she raised her gaze from the tantalizing view his open collar offered, past the strong shape of his chin to his dark eyes. "I confess, Officer. Guilty as charged."

"Why?"

"Aw, come on, Hawk. You know Myrtle. She's been telling the same busybody stories for years." Gossip that had driven both Beth and her older sister Marilee out of town, each in their turn. "This time I thought I'd give her something really juicy to talk about." It had been an impish impulse, probably a result of her long flight west, and weeks of fatigue, plus a degree of residual anger, she admitted, for the way the town had treated her years ago. "No harm done."

"Of course not." He rolled his tongue along the inside of his cheek, and her gaze was pulled to his lips— lips that were artistically drawn in fine, sensuous lines. "I don't suppose you'd know anything about folks thinking you were going to start a massage parlor here at your grandmother's house."

She stifled a laugh. Jake at the service station ran a close second to Myrtle in spreading the word. "Well, people around here do work hard. It seemed like there might be a market—"

"I'll be the first customer in line." Hawk raised a single, raven eyebrow. "Naturally the city council may have some concerns about zoning regulations. As they would about you starting a home for unwed mothers."

"Millie Russell across the street—"

"I'm really worried about you starting a strip joint in the old movie theater on Main Street, though. That might attract a bad crowd."

"I didn't!"

"Then there are the nude paintings..."

A laugh chortled up from her throat. "You're kidding." Things had really gotten out of hand.

"And New York Bohemian groupies camping out in the backyard."

"No! I don't believe—"

He cupped his hand along the column of her neck, sliding his tapered, callused fingers beneath the heavy weight of her blond hair. With a quick intake of air, she caught his scent, a rich, masculine mix of leather and the open range. "I've missed you, Beth. Welcome home."

His baritone voice skidded along her spine and curled into a spot near her heart, a place she hadn't even realized was empty. "It's good to see you, too, Hawk." Her pulse throbbed beneath his palm.

He was the last person she should be glad to see, she realized, struggling against the painful wrenching sensation in her chest. The one person whose betrayal had hurt the most.

She slipped away from his touch.

"So how come you're a deputy sheriff? Whatever happened to Harvard?" Her pride wouldn't allow him to see how his casual touch affected her or the way her hand trembled as she drank a sip of cola to steady her nerves. She was no longer a fifteen-year-old girl madly infatuated with a college man home on summer vacation, she reminded herself.

"I graduated and then went on to finish law school."

"Times have to be tough if you couldn't land a job." He'd been a top student at Newellton Union High. She was equally confident he'd done well at Harvard.

"Actually I had so many offers I could hardly sort them out. I'd done pretty well. I was on the *Law Review*." Beth suspected he was being modest. Knowing Hawk he'd probably been the editor.

He lifted the sheer curtain over the sink and looked out into the neighbor's yard. Angular rays of sunlight filtered through the brilliant yellow leaves of a poplar tree, dappling shadows across a screened back porch. A power mower hummed from somewhere nearby. "I finally picked a very prestigious law firm in New York City."

An ache twisted in Beth's chest. Hawk had been in New York. If the fates had meant for them to meet again, she would have bumped into him on the street. Or he could have asked Grandma Claire for her phone number, a disappointed voice reminded her.

Hawk turned from the view of the neighbor's yard. "After about a year I decided law wasn't right for me. So I came back to the land of my ancestors."

"As a cop." She smiled at his reference to the land in which he'd always felt great pride.

"Cop. Social worker. Mediator. Occasionally a marriage counselor." His broad shoulders lifted in a modest gesture that somehow managed to convey both the authority of his position and the pleasure he found in his work. "It's a living."

"You work here in Newellton?"

"Yeah. The town council, in its wisdom, decided they could save money by contracting for police services from the county. It works out fine for me." He let his warm gaze settle over her again, bringing a little flutter to her stomach. "How 'bout you? You like your job?"

"I love illustrating. That's what I studied at the Art Center—not stripping." She grinned. "It's the stress and constant deadlines that drive you nutsy in the advertising business. And the crazy clients. Can you imagine animated paper towels? The president of the company insisted that's what he wanted, so that's what he got." Her laugh came from low in her throat. "I've been going out of my way to buy the competitor's product ever since we got the account."

Amusement sparked in his dark eyes. "And here I'd thought of loyalty as one of your finest attributes," he mocked.

"In spite of my best efforts I just couldn't get emotional about Winifred Wipe-Up." Beth could have been loyal to Hawk, she recalled. But he'd turned his back on her devotion all because of a few spiteful remarks made by the town's Gossiping Gerdies.

If she had good sense she'd ask him to leave right now. Then she could get on with sorting through her grandmother's personal effects and work her way up to tackling the overflowing attic of a confirmed pack rat. There was no reason to spend any more time in Newellton, with all of its memories, than was absolutely necessary.

She lifted her gaze to Hawk's. In that moment she realized his casual stance and easy manner were all an act. Finding him standing at her grandmother's front door should have warned her, she thought with belated awareness. The tilt of his determined chin and the smoky look in his eyes gave him away. He wasn't here to check if she was about to start a strip joint in town. In the next few seconds he was going to say something that would have sounded like heaven ten years ago. Now she didn't want to hear it at all.

She closed her eyes and made it to a mental count of three before he said, "Rumor also has it you only have peanut butter in the house for dinner. How 'bout steak and fries at the coffee shop. I'm buying."

She expelled the breath she'd been holding. Heaven had come too late. "I don't think that's a good idea."

"You're on a straight diet of peanut butter and junk food?" With lifted eyebrows he slowly perused the shape of her breasts, her narrow waist and the length of her legs snugged into tight-fitting jeans. "If that's the case, you're definitely getting good results."

She fought off the heat that raced to her cheeks and the throbbing sensation she felt much lower in her body. "Hawk, we gave everybody in town plenty to talk about ten years ago. I'm not interested in going all through that again."

"We're both a lot older now."

"I'm going to be gone in two weeks, and I plan never to come back again."

His eyes narrowed ever so slightly. "Then it's your charitable duty to give the townspeople a legacy of conversation to keep them going through the long, dark winter."

"You're crazy, you know that?" But the offer was tempting, according to the devilish little imp who'd been sitting on her shoulder all afternoon. She simply wouldn't let the fact that Hawk was a hundred eighty pounds of totally masculine persuasion influence her. "You'll ruin your reputation hanging around with me," she warned.

"I'm willing to risk it." Hawk tucked his fingertips into his hip pockets and gave her his most confident smile. Ten years ago he hadn't dared spend any more time with Beth Haggerty. He'd been all hormones, hungry for Beth like he'd never been for any woman before or since. What he'd had in mind would have gotten him tarred and feathered in almost any county in the state. Beth had been too damn young, and he'd been a long way from being ready to make a permanent commitment.

But Beth had grown up. Very nicely, he mentally added with another appreciative look. Maybe he had, too.

He remembered the first time he'd noticed her around town. A couple of teenage hoodlums had her trapped in the parking lot of the bank. They were up to no good. And she was standing them off with a stick, her emerald green eyes flashing with as much outraged passion and fury as she could muster. It might have been a little dumb, since he was badly outnumbered, but Hawk had waded into the mess. He figured a girl who probably weighed no more than a hundred pounds right after a big meal could use some help. He'd since decided she was feisty enough to have managed on her own. Probably.

Still, he'd walked her safely home and discovered a courage in her that would have impressed his Crow ancestors. She was doggedly fighting the losing battle of a reputation for being loose and easy that her sister had earned, not Beth.

That day, at least, she'd counted many coups on her enemies. One of the guys had bruises to show for his taunts. Hawk imagined if she'd been a brave in his grandfather's village she would have earned the right to wear a few eagle feathers in the wild tumble of her blond curls.

He smiled at the thought and picked up his hat from the kitchen table, wondering what she'd done with the feathers he'd given her.

At the moment, however, he was far more interested in determining just what it would take to get Beth to stay in Newellton for a long, long time.

Just as she stepped off the porch, with Hawk right behind her, Beth caught the subtle movement of window curtains in the house across the street. Millie Russell might have been Grandma Claire's oldest and dearest friend, but she gave new meaning to the expression "neighborhood watch." Everybody within a two-block radius had better mind their p's and q's or Millie would have the word spread all around town quicker than a prairie fire could leap across a county road.

Like most of the houses along the street, the Russell place was two stories topped by attic dormers. Asphalt shingles, wood siding painted white and trimmed in shades of blue or green, and porches that ran the width of the house were the norm. Here and there a modern one-story house added a jarring note.

"Hang on a minute, Hawk." She adjusted the cable-knit sweater she'd thrown around her shoulders, knowing the evening would turn cool before they returned from dinner. She'd also taken the time to slip on an oversize blouse to cover her tank top and tied the ends of the shirt at her waist. With less flesh bared to Hawk's scrutiny she felt a little more in control of the situation. "I've got to talk to Millie Russell's grandson about mowing the grass till I get Grandma's house sold."

"Or the snow flies."

"True. Then he could keep the sidewalk shoveled." She strolled across the street to the boy who was raking up the last of the grass clippings from the lawn he'd just mowed. A light breeze tinged with the expectation of autumn carried the rich scent of new-mown grass. "Hi, Tommy, you were about waist-high the last time I saw you. You've grown."

He was all adolescent arms, legs and acne, and his face flushed a bright hue. "'Lo, Miss Haggerty."

Lord, the kid really knew how to make a twenty-five-year-old woman feel ancient. *Miss Haggerty,* indeed. He probably put her right up there with Grandma Millie—one foot in the grave.

"I need someone to mow the grass regularly and rake up the leaves. Do you think you'd have time? I could pay you a little something."

"Gosh, sure, Miss Haggerty. I can always use a few extra bucks." He gave her a shy smile. "Could I start tomorrow? I kinda got a...well, you know. Tonight's not real good. And it'll be dark soon."

"Tomorrow's fine, Tommy. I'll pay you a little extra the first time because the grass is so long." How her grandmother had managed to mow her own grass all these years was nothing less than amazing. Perhaps that was why she'd been so healthy until a sudden heart attack took her at eighty-five. Not a bad way to go, Beth concluded for about the millionth time. It was just the way Grandma had hoped—though the knowledge didn't reduce Beth's grief a great deal. She would always miss knowing that Grandma Claire was only a phone call away.

"I'll come over right after school tomorrow."

She thanked him and crossed the gravel street back to where Hawk waited for her next to his car, a black-and-white Jeep wagon with four-wheel drive, a strip of red and amber lights across the top and an undercarriage that rode high to clear rough terrain.

Beneath the civilized veneer of his sheriff's uniform she could still see the Indian brave Hawk would have been a hundred years ago. As a girl she'd once sketched him sitting tall and magnificent on a pony, his bow and arrow aimed at a buffalo. Her fingers itched now to draw him again, to catch just the right shade for his sun-burnished skin, to highlight the fascinating bold angles and planes of his face and shape the rugged lines of his muscular body gleaming with sweat and straining in pursuit of his quarry.

Perhaps after she returned to New York she'd find the time—some night when her memories made her sleepless with their infinitely varied textures and vivid colors.

When she reached the car, she glanced back over her shoulder. The shadow was still there in the window watching the street, just as she had expected.

The little elf she'd been listening to all day tweaked her again.

She waved at the shadow, turned, stood on tiptoe and planted a very firm kiss on Hawk's smooth cheek.

Gotcha, Millie!

Chapter Two

"You're determined to keep their tongues wagging, aren't you?"

"I guess that was a bit childish of me," Beth admitted with a sigh. She didn't know what had gotten into her since she'd arrived in Newellton, and she certainly hadn't expected to feel such an incredible jolt of longing when she'd kissed Hawk. It was supposed to have been a joke. Something deep inside her had reacted in a far different way. The *gotcha* had been hers, not Millie Russell's.

"How 'bout you count me out of your next little prank. I don't appreciate being kissed by a woman just to make a point." Though he hadn't yet backed out of the driveway, his hands clasped the steering wheel so tightly his knuckles were white; his jaw was set in a tense, angry line.

My God, she'd embarrassed him. She hadn't even thought...

"I'm sorry, Hawk. It won't happen again. I'll be on my best behavior when I'm with you." In fact, kissing Hawk was not a good plan under any circumstances. Beth didn't want to take a whole new set of painful memories back with her when she returned to the city. Nor did she want to jeopardize his position in the town.

"You've got to give these folks a chance, Beth. They aren't trying to hurt you."

"They destroyed my sister," she reminded him grimly, "and painted me with the same dirty brush. All I wanted was to be accepted for myself." I wanted you to see me as I really was, she silently added, not as others told you.

"Every time you thought they messed up, you got defensive. Then you pulled some prank that only managed to confirm the gossip."

"I fought back as best I could. What was I supposed to do? Smile sweetly when some guy claimed he'd gone to bed with me? Or laugh it off when Myrtle Symington squealed to Grandma that I hadn't been going to drill team practice?"

He switched on the ignition and shifted into reverse. "Where had you been?"

"At the library." Hiding.

Slanting her a glance, he said, "That doesn't sound like a major criminal offense. Why didn't you tell your grandmother where you were?"

She leaned her elbow on the open window sill and looked straight ahead, ignoring the way the breeze whipped strands of her hair across her face. "Grandma desperately wanted me to be popular in school. She thought by being on the drill team I could live down my sister's reputation . . . but it didn't work out that way."

"You want to tell me about it?"

The persuasive gentleness of his voice nearly undid Beth, along with the painful wash of memories. She blinked away the burning sensation at the back of her eyes.

"I went to the tryouts at the beginning of the school year. Like I was supposed to. I'd practiced all of the routines for hours and hours. Alone, of course, because I didn't have anyone to help me. When I showed up at the gym . . ." She ran her fingertip along the felt weather stripping of the window. She could still feel the hurt and confusion of that autumn after Hawk had gone back to Harvard without even saying good-bye. God, it had been hell to be a teenager. "The girls were all standing together in a bunch under the basketball hoop. Every once in a while one would look my direction and then they'd all giggle. I knew they were talking about me, and I simply couldn't handle it."

"Did you ever think they were as nervous about tryouts as you were? Maybe that's why they were giggling."

She frowned. That possibility hadn't ever crossed her mind. "It didn't seem like it at the time."

"So you ran."

"To the library. Or sometimes out in the country where I could sketch anything that caught my eye. I always managed to get home about the time I would have if I'd been on the team."

"And when your grandmother found out?"

Beth smiled. "She told me I had a real inborn talent for art and that I should draw every chance I got."

"So that's when you decided to paint the caricature of Myrtle on the plate-glass window at the grocery store. My mother wrote me about that escapade." His deep-throated laugh was like a warm, sheltering blanket across Beth's past. "I always wondered what made you do it."

"I grant you it was a dumb stunt but I was so mad. I was just a kid," she pointed out, though that hardly qualified as an excuse to vandalize someone's property. She grinned to herself, aware her remorse still didn't run very deep for what amounted to a harmless prank. "You have to admit Myrtle's nose really does look like a hen's beak. And her eyes are terribly beady. A flesh-and-blood character right out of a cartoon strip."

"Not a kind way to see her, but true enough," he conceded, the corner of his mouth twitching into a smile.

The cool air blowing in the car window carried the scent of sage from the land just beyond the borders of town, along with the distinctive smell of recently harvested wheat. For a New Yorker that was at least a refreshing change and so achingly familiar Beth had to fight off a wave of nostalgia. Not all of the memories of growing up in Newellton were bad. Her little escapade painting Myrtle's window had gotten her a lot of attention from the high school art teacher—along with a month's worth of being grounded by her grandmother and a full Saturday of washing every one of Myrtle's windows, top to bottom.

"I want you to know I haven't had an urge to graffiti a single window since I moved to New York." In fact, away from the office she led an incredibly bor-

ing social life, though she doubted anyone in Newellton would believe that.

Chuckling softly, Hawk wheeled the car left onto
Main Street. "Glad to hear it. I'd hate to have to haul
you off to jail." Though come to think of it, the idea
held a certain appeal. If Beth got in a kissing mood
again, he would a whole lot rather they had some privacy.

The unexpected feel of her lips had really knocked
him back on his heels. Then when he realized she'd
kissed him to show off for the neighbors, he'd been
rocked again, this time by disappointment. Hard
woman to understand.

She'd always kept him guessing. He recalled when
she'd insisted more than once that they take a quick
dip in the river, with all their clothes on, thank God.
Or when she'd simply wanted to lie on her back and
watch the clouds. Then she would be up and running
again, so filled with the joy of living he could hardly
keep up. And smiling. Beth always made him smile.

With a practiced eye he checked out the businesses
on Main Street as he cruised by—the Five-and-Dime
was closed for the night, the drugstore would stay open
till nine as would Myrtle's grocery. The largest estab-
lishment in town was the old hardware store formerly
owned by Beth's father. Everyone still referred to it as
"Hank's place" although he'd died and the business
had been sold almost twenty years ago. In Newellton
it took more than one generation to belong.

Even as a kid, Hawk had worked hard to be accepted as part of the community.

"You know, it's really strange," Beth said
thoughtfully.

"What's that?" In the rearview mirror he kept his eye on an old Chevy filled with teenagers from the Indian reservation out on an evening prowl. Except for a recent rash of house break-ins, there wasn't much crime in Newellton. Still, it paid to stay alert.

"If anybody was going to be the town rebel, it should have been you. Right off the reservation. A father who ended up in the drunk tank every weekend. Instead, I was the one with the hellion reputation."

"I was rebelling."

"Come on! Straight A's in high school. A scholarship to Harvard. That hardly qualifies for Rebel of the Year."

"My parents sure thought so." He gave her a wink. "Only you white-eyes didn't know what I was up to."

She threw a halfhearted punch that grazed his arm, and he laughed. Lord, how he loved her spunk.

A half-dozen curious heads turned when they entered the Roundup Café. Beth pulled back her shoulders slightly and lifted her chin. The last she'd heard, it wasn't a crime to have dinner with the local deputy sheriff.

The place hadn't changed a bit in the past ten years, or the past twenty-five, she mentally corrected. The same ageless orange vinyl covered the counter stools and booth benches. The telltale odor of fried food hung in the air as it always had. Even the daily specials headlined on the mirror behind the ever-steaming coffeepots appeared unchanged.

Hawk clamped a friendly hand on the shoulder of a middle-aged man sitting at the counter.

"How's it going, Leroy?" he asked.

"No cause to complain." His leathery, weather-lined face cracked into a smile.

"You having any trouble with folks rushing the hunting season out your way?"

"Well, now..." He settled his spoon into a big dish of chili smothered with cheese and onions. "Did hear a couple a rifle shots long 'bout last Tuesday. Didn't think much of it at the time."

"I'll ask the game warden to keep an eye out your direction."

"Appreciate it. Half the time them fool hunters cain't see no difference twixt a cow and a buck."

As though taking roll, Hawk greeted the next man seated at the counter. Beth had little choice but to wait patiently for him to finish his business, all the while aware of the two women at a booth nearby. Between bites of chocolate sundaes, they eyed her and whispered across the table. She recognized one as the mother of a classmate—a girl who'd been on the drill team as well as popular with the football players. She wondered what had happened to Playful Pamela Perkins but didn't want to ask.

"How 'bout you, Charlie?" Hawk asked the second man. "Keepin' out of trouble?"

"Yeah, I am, but you might want to drop out my way Friday nights. The kids have taken to drag racing along Avenue E."

"I'll cruise by next Friday for sure. See if we can slow them down a bit. Thanks for letting me know."

With a "See you later" Hawk took Beth's elbow in a proprietary gesture. She loved the heated feel of his hand through her cotton blouse, but the public display of his possessiveness made her want to cringe. Please, she thought, not in front of half the town, unless you want the news to spread faster than a speeding bullet.

Instead of heading for the inconspicuous rear booth, Hawk ushered her to one right up front where everyone who walked in the door would get a good look at the two of them sitting together. He was definitely a glutton for punishment. The local gossips would have a heyday.

So be it, she thought, sliding to the center of the vinyl bench. She had nothing to be ashamed of.

"Sorry for the interruption," he said as he sat down across from her.

"Do you know everybody in town?"

"It's my job. I've got better than a hundred square miles to patrol on my own. The best way to do that is to let the good folks around here be my eyes and ears." He smiled, and sun-burnished crinkles formed at the corners of his dark eyes. "My ancestors used to listen to the land so they could hunt successfully. I'm just doing the same thing. Only I listen to people, not the howl of wolves."

"I'd think wolves would be more reliable," she mumbled.

With a wry smile, he shook his head and slid a menu from behind the napkin holder. "I recommend the New York steak. Definitely not the chili."

"It did look potent, didn't it?" she said, and laughed. Hawk looked potent, too. So casually virile it took her breath away.

A young girl with the fresh face of a local homecoming queen—bouncy ponytail included—arrived with coffee, mugs and silverware.

"Evening, Annie Mae," Hawk said as she poured the coffee. "How're the steaks tonight?"

"Same as always, Mr. Hawk." Smiling, she pulled her pencil from her apron pocket. "Well-done, with fries?"

"That'll do for both of us."

"Actually, could I have mine medium rare?" Beth asked. "With maybe lettuce and sliced tomatoes instead of fries?"

"Sure." The girl jotted down the order.

Hawk waited until she'd finished taking the order. "I heard you were in charge of the decorations for the next dance at the high school, Annie Mae."

"Yeah. And I haven't a clue what to do. Everybody's sick of Western stuff. And half the time the guys won't dance once they're there. Claim they don't know how. If you've got any ideas—"

"You ought to ask Beth." He nodded across the table. "She used to decorate the gym when she went to Newellton High."

Beth's head snapped up. "I'm not going to be around—"

"Really?" Annie Mae's dark eyes rounded eagerly. "I could sure use some help. I've got a committee and all, but none of us can think of anything different, I mean *really* different, for that dumb gym. It's just such a yucky place to have a dance anyway, and they won't let us go as far as the county seat, or anything fun like that."

Beth remembered decorating the gym more than once practically by herself, and then being so tired she was almost glad she didn't have a date for the dance. All the guys had either wanted to get into her pants or were scared to death to talk to her.

Annie Mae was lucky to have a committee, however lacking in original ideas they might be. "The secret's in having a good theme and creating some kind of a false ceiling," she suggested. "Then it doesn't feel so much like a gym."

"But how? The dance is a week from Saturday. Could you maybe talk to us...give us some ideas?"

Feeling torn between wanting to help and knowing she shouldn't, Beth lined up her silverware in a neat row on the paper napkin. She didn't want to get drawn back into the town of Newellton, with all of the infighting and cattiness. Annie Mae looked like she was the most popular, and probably the prettiest, girl in school. It wouldn't help her to be known as a friend of Beth Haggerty. Hawk should have known better than to suggest the idea.

"I'm sorry," she said. "I've got an awful lot of work to do to clear out my grandmother's house. I just don't see how I'd have the time."

The girl's shoulders sagged. "Oh, well...if you think of anything..." She turned and walked back behind the counter to place their order.

Hawk reached across the table and covered Beth's hand. He'd hoped by offering a chance to help Annie Mae he could get Beth to see that the town wasn't all that bad. His ploy hadn't worked, but he wasn't about to give up just yet.

"Would it have taken all that much time to give them some ideas?" he asked, his voice coaxing. "It's not every day those kids can get advice from a professional artist from New York."

"Hawk, I don't belong in Newellton. I never have. I just want to get Grandma's house cleaned up and get out of here."

He wasn't going to let that happen. Not till she'd given Newellton, and him, a fair chance to change her mind. "You know, Annie Mae's a real interesting girl," Hawk continued as if he hadn't heard her. "She lives with her father in a trailer he squatted on some vacant land over near Running Creek. Her old man drinks too much. He put her mom in the hospital more than once with bruises and a couple of broken bones. Couple of years ago she died. Just gave up trying, I guess. Her dad can't hold a job, not that he tries very hard."

Hawk glanced to the counter where the girl was working. "Annie Mae is different. Good grades. Real active in school. And still manages to work here five nights a week, probably supporting her dad. She's the kind of kid I'd like to see make it in this world."

"Decorating the gym for a dance does *not* make or break a person in life."

He leveled her a very steady gaze. "Having a friend who's made it...in spite of what the town expected of her...can."

Beth felt herself sinking into the vinyl seat. He sure knew how to lay guilt on a person. If he would just take his hand away from hers maybe she could think more clearly. His skin was a dozen shades darker than hers, his hand big and strong and roughened by weather, when it should be as soft as that of a New York attorney. She admitted she liked him better this way, a man of the land—tough and enduring.

She blew out a breath and slipped her hand into her lap. "All right. I'll see what I can do—if I can find the time."

His smile was both sweet and triumphant at once.

Damn him! Hawk wasn't going to lure her back into the small-town web she'd been so desperate to leave. As much as she might ache for Annie Mae and the situation the girl faced, she wasn't a social worker. No way.

She glanced out the window as two battered pickup trucks rumbled by, one filled with fencing material and the other full of hay, their headlights cutting through the dim light of scattered street lamps. When was the last time, she wondered, that she'd seen a pickup truck rolling down Fifth Avenue? Not ever, that she could recall. But out here a truck was the vehicle of choice. A working vehicle. Not a taxi. And not some flashy, expensive car that required an equal fortune to garage it somewhere nearby. Definitely down-home Western-style. Comfortable. The more dings in the fenders the better.

Odd how after all these years she missed the sight of well-used trucks more than anything else. Except, perhaps, Hawk.

She remembered his old truck more than any other. How they'd parked at the end of a dark road that stretched into the empty prairie. The night sounds of crickets. The awkwardness of the front seat. The press of the door handle on the small of her back. How the windows had steamed in response to their youthful passion.

Lord, she didn't dare think about that.

The clatter of dishes placed on a Formica tabletop accompanied the arrival of their sizzling steaks. For a few moments they ate in silence, Beth acutely aware of Hawk's nearness, the movement of his hands, the strength of his tapered fingers and her own desire to feel them touching her again. Just like everything else about the man, she was sure Hawk would be a careful, confident lover. More than once over the years she'd wished they had made love truly and completely on one of those wild summer nights out on the prairie. But Hawk's willpower and principles would never let things go too far.

"I gather you eat here often," Beth said, determined to get her mind off the single track it had been following since Hawk had arrived at her door.

"Most nights. I just rent a room over the beauty shop for now. I've got a hot plate, microwave and one of those apartment refrigerators. I don't do a lot of cooking."

"Sounds lonely." But not much different from the way she lived in a cramped walk-up apartment in the city.

"It's a place to sleep. Don't need it for much more than that. I bought twenty acres north of town and plan to start building a house there next spring. Assuming I can get a loan."

"You're really laying down roots in Newellton." She ignored a twinge of envy and cut another bite of steak that was cooked just right with a nice pink center.

"My roots have always been here, Beth. I just didn't recognize that when I was a kid."

She had no sense of belonging at all, Beth realized, either here or in New York. "Are you going to ranch?"

"Maybe raise some horses. Mostly I want to be sure I'll always have open space around me." He doused his French fries with ketchup. "My apartment was so small in New York I could hear the guy next door snore."

She laughed and pushed her untamed hair back from her face. "I know what you mean. There must be a rule in New York that they can't build walls thicker than paper. More than once I've gotten up in the night to turn on the TV so I wouldn't have to listen to my neighbor's love life in all of its breathless detail.''

"How 'bout you, Beth?" He held his knife poised above his steak and studied her with a dark, intense gaze across the table. "Anyone special in your life?"

"No. No one special." She let her gaze drop to her plate. The only man she'd ever thought of in that way had been Hawk. And he'd left her with only a few youthful memories of kisses and caresses that she couldn't quite get out of her mind. "It's hard to meet guys in a big city. Unless you're into the bar scene or there's someone at work. Mostly it's a series of awkward blind dates set up by well-intentioned friends." She lifted her eyes again and grinned. "I've had some real doozies, believe me."

The door opened and with it came a gust of sage-scented air to war momentarily with the aroma of fried onions. Tommy Russell, his hair freshly combed and his shirt tucked into his jeans, made a beeline for Annie Mae. From the look of adoration in the girl's eyes, Tommy could have been Adonis. When she slipped her arm around his slender waist and lifted her face for a quick kiss, Beth felt a million years old. Had she ever looked at any man like that? Not recently. Not since she'd been fifteen years old.

When she glanced back at Hawk she was snared by his dark gaze. The muscles in her stomach tightened. Everything she'd felt about him ten years ago was still there. The ache. The need.

It was no more than hormones and childish infatuation, she told herself sternly.

And it was too damn late. Hawk was rooted in Newellton. She was a tumbleweed that had been blown

a long way down the road. She could never come back.
Never.

A few moments later the women at the neighboring
table left. Mrs. Parker gave Beth a tight little smile,
and she nodded in return. No, Beth would never be
welcome in Newellton.

As the women exited, a man entered the diner, taking a seat at the counter. He wore dirty overalls. Gen-
erally unkempt, his beard was at least three days old.

Without saying a word, Annie Mae poured the
stranger a cup of coffee and a moment later dished up
a bowl of chili, which she placed in front of him.

"That's her father," Hawk said in a low voice.

"Annie Mae's?"

"Yeah. At least he appears sober tonight."

How hard for the girl, Beth thought, realizing the
reason Hawk felt a special kinship with the young
woman. He'd experienced the same sort of dysfunc-
tional family in his young life. Little wonder Hawk
was eager for her to help out the girl.

Hawk barely tasted the last few bites of his steak.
He was concentrating too hard on Beth Haggerty to be
interested in any flavor except hers. At least he'd
learned there wasn't some guy in New York she'd be
eager to return to. The window of opportunity stood
wide open if he could figure a way to get past the defensive barriers she'd erected long ago.

Her green eyes, dotted with golden lights, still held
that spark of barely suppressed devilment he remembered. Her lips were so mobile they always appeared
to be on the verge of a smile, as though asking the
world to give her a chance to have a little fun. Her
thick mane of curls could stand confinement no more
than the woman herself. "Mischief" was her middle

name. Somehow she used that wonderful attribute to keep the whole town of Newellton at a safe distance. What a waste.

Finished with his meal, Hawk glanced at his watch. "Mind if we take a little cruise around town? Whenever you're done. There've been some house break-ins lately and I need to keep my eyes out for any unusual activity."

"No problem," she said, shoving her empty plate away.

He dropped a generous tip on the table for Annie Mae and paid the bill at the cash register.

Just as he held open the door for Beth, a mud-spattered Cadillac slid into the first parking slot. Hawk stifled a groan. Small-town politics were not the part of his job he liked best.

"Evening, Mr. Mayor," he said as a man with a physique resembling a half-melted snowman levered himself out of the car.

Taylor Franklin slid his arms into his suit jacket, concealing the suspenders that kept his pants in place. "Hello, Hawk. Peaceful tonight?"

"So far as I know, sir."

"Didn't see many cars at the tavern when I went by, so maybe it'll stay that way." His gaze shifted to Beth, and his puffy eyes narrowed. "Heard you were back in town."

From his tone, Beth had the distinct impression he'd just announced the town was being overrun with rodents.

"Understand you're planning to start a business here," the mayor said.

Wondering which of the rumors he'd heard, Beth gave him her brightest smile. "Are you interested in investing a little capital in a sure thing?"

Color rose to his cheeks. "I think not, Miss Haggerty. I will be more than pleased, however, to list your grandmother's house whenever you are prepared to sell."

Over my dead body, she thought. She'd list with a Realtor in Helena before she'd give Taylor Franklin a dime of commission. More than anyone else, this was the man who had driven her sister out of town. All because he thought his son had been too good for Marilee.

"I would have thought, Your Honor, that the mayor would be interested in bringing new businesses into town," she said. "Good for the economy and all that."

"Remember, the city council will have to approve any business license—"

"You're not suggesting they'd deny a town native—"

Hawk placed a silencing arm around Beth's shoulders. "I'm afraid you've been listening to unfounded rumors, Taylor. She's not planning to start any business here at all."

Taylor waited for Beth to confirm Hawk's statement. When she didn't speak, the mayor said, "I hope you're right, Hawk. And I also think a young man of your caliber and with a fine future ahead of him ought to be careful whose company he keeps."

Hawk felt Beth's back stiffen. "If you'll excuse us, sir, I have to get out on patrol."

He ushered her around the side of the café to where he had parked his car. Dammit, Beth wasn't even making an effort. If she'd just give the town a little slack they'd accept her.

"Why didn't you tell him the truth?" he asked more gruffly than he had intended as he unlocked the Jeep's door.

"Why should I?" She held herself very straight, but in the dim light of the parking lot he caught the tremble of her lower lip. "The only kind of truth Taylor Franklin has ever believed was his own version. Facts would only confuse his small, narrow-minded brain."

"All you had to do was tell him the real reason you came back."

"You're mad at me again, aren't you? And ashamed to be seen with me."

He grabbed her by both shoulders and spun her around to face him. His fingers kneaded into the thickness of her sweater. "You're damn right I'm mad at you. But don't you ever, *ever* think I'm ashamed of being with you. That's never been true. And it isn't now."

Beth trembled. She wanted to believe him. Instead her head was filled with Franklin's last words as though they were daggers out of the past—the past she'd inherited, however unwillingly, from Marilee.

"Did you ever know my sister, Hawk?"

Chapter Three

"Marilee was a year or two ahead of me in school." Hawk climbed into the Jeep on the driver's side. "Yeah, I knew of her."

"Everyone did. By reputation." Beth snapped her seat belt in place as Hawk switched on the ignition and backed out of the parking lot.

"I suppose. You never talked much about her."

She'd never known quite what to say. "She wasn't an angel. Not by a long shot. I really think when our father died it hit her harder than it did me. Left her at loose ends. Maybe because she was just beginning to notice boys and didn't quite know what to do about them." Beth knitted her fingers tightly together in her lap. After all these years, it was still hard to talk about the sister she'd blindly adored. Even with a man like Hawk, who was the best listener she'd ever known. "By the time Marilee got to high school, she was ready to explode. Grandma Claire didn't have much control over her.''

"Kids rebel in different ways.''

"Along about the end of her junior year she settled down. She and Bud Franklin had something really good going together.''

He raised his raven eyebrows. "The mayor's son?''

"The same.'' The car slowly cruised down a side street. Beth recalled most of the houses with their big trees and neatly trimmed lawns. She remembered some of the families and wondered if they still lived in the same houses. Probably. Nothing much changed in Newellton. "Mr. Franklin got wind of their relationship. He blew a gasket. Told Bud if he had anything more to do with Marilee he'd send him away to school. So they resorted to sneaking around to see each other. In a place this small, it was inevitable Bud's father would hear about it.''

"I gather he was not pleased.''

"There was a terrible scene at our house. I thought Grandma Claire was going to have a stroke, she got so mad at Mr. Franklin. She didn't want to listen to anything bad about Marilee. Franklin told her—'' Beth glanced at Hawk, her heart catching at the sight of his distinctive profile. So bold. So primitive. Her fingers itched to release the thong that held his hair in place. She wanted to see the dark strands blow free, touch their wildness. But she couldn't do that.

"Franklin said Bud had a marvelous future in front of him, and he wouldn't let some snip of a girl mess everything up for his son.''

A chuckle slipped up from deep in Hawk's throat.

"It isn't a laughing matter, Hawk. Franklin used almost the same words tonight when he told you to stay away from me. He could ruin you."

"Let me worry about that." He reached across the car and placed his hand lightly on Beth's arm. Heat radiated out from his touch. When she tried to pull away, he squeezed gently, shooting a rush of warmth right to the hyper-sensitive flesh of her inner elbow. She fought off the sensation.

"Bud's future, as the mayor called it," Hawk reported, "has turned out to be limited to working as assistant manager for the local ice-cream shop. He's married to one of the Parker girls—"

"Pamela?"

"I think so. They've got four or five kids, and I've never once seen them dressed in anything except hand-me-downs."

Beth wanted to gloat. Just a little. But it seemed pointless after all this time. "You still don't understand. Taylor Franklin has always been the most influential man in this town. The whole county listens when he coughs. If he decides you're unworthy of being a deputy, because you've been seen cavorting with me, then you're history."

He slanted her an amused glance. "Cavorting?"

"Whatever." Pointedly she lifted his hand away and placed it back on the steering wheel. Immediately the cool autumn air seeped back in through her sweater. She shivered. "Taylor Franklin keeps his promises. Within days of that confrontation, Bud was gone. We learned later he'd been sent to a military school in Idaho."

"What happened to Marilee?"

"She moped around for a few weeks. Everyone in town gave her the cold shoulder. The word of her fallen-woman status had obviously been spread. By Franklin and Myrtle, and Millie Russell, I suppose. God knows who else. Then she realized she was pregnant."

"That's rough." He wheeled up another residential street.

"Shortly after that she ran away." Rough did not come close to expressing how much Beth had missed her sister, sibling squabbles over the bathroom included. "About three years later Grandma heard from her at Christmas. She called from Los Angeles. She didn't talk long. Just enough to say she was okay. We never knew what happened to the baby... or to Marilee."

"I'm sorry about your sister. I really am. But nothing about her has anything to do with us."

"There is no *us*, Hawk. Except for a few brief months when we—I—was a kid, there never has been."

He pulled up to a curb, shifted into neutral and switched off the headlights. The dial on the police radio under the dashboard glowed in the darkness. "That's not how I saw it, Beth." His voice strained with a huskiness that rasped against her flesh, setting each of her nerve endings on fire.

She swallowed hard. "Then why..." Did she have the courage to ask? After all these years, could it possibly make a difference? His betrayal had hurt so much. "One day you were there. We were together. A couple. The next thing I knew, you were gone. Someone must have said something... warned you about me. Told you I'd ruin your life."

Shifting his position, he draped his arm across the back of the seat. His fingers played lightly with the tips of her hair. She sensed more than experienced the sensation, almost as though his touch was no more than an illusion. A dream she'd had more than once.

"I'm sorry you thought that. It wasn't true. The fact is I took the coward's way out."

"I don't understand."

"I was running scared, Beth."

"A big, brave guy like you, scared of little ol' me?" she mocked, letting the hurt show in spite of herself.

"Of the things you made me feel. The things you made me want. I was determined to show everybody that an Indian off the reservation could make it, really make it, in the white man's world. I was going to climb to the top of the heap, whatever it took." His hand slipped beneath her hair, palming the back of her neck. His fingers kneaded gently. "I knew if I saw you again, we would make love together. Once wouldn't have been enough. I knew that, too. Then I'd never get back to Harvard or go to law school or do anything except love you again and again because I wouldn't have ever been able to leave you."

Tears stung at the back of Beth's eyes. His words had come too late. No one could change the past. "You could have called..."

"And said what? You were so damn young. Had so much life in front of you. How could I tie you down? I didn't want you to miss all those high school dances. Or the dates I knew you'd have."

She laughed a bittersweet sound. "Oh, Hawk, the whole time I went to Newellton High I went to only one dance. It was a disaster. After the dance the guy took me out to Lovers' Gulch on Hopkins Road. We parked and I had to fight him off. He kept telling me Marilee had always put out for his older brother, so why wouldn't I? I ended up walking home.''

Hawk muttered a curse. ''I'm sorry, Beth. God, I'm sorry.''

Someone switched on a porch light, and the lawn next to the car was bathed in a yellow glow. Winter-mulched flower beds circled the grass in a necklace of hay-covered mounds. A screen door creaked open.

''Looks like Newellton's Neighborhood Watch is on full alert,'' Beth said. ''We'd better keep moving or somebody will report you to the sheriff. You wouldn't want word about how you spend your time to get back to the mayor.'' The best thing she could do for Hawk would be to leave town as quickly as possible. For herself, she'd simply have to put her memories back in some quiet niche and forget them all over again.

Straightening, Hawk shifted the car into gear and eased away from the curb.

You could tell a lot about a town by listening to the night sounds. He'd learned to tell the difference between a dog barking for the sheer joy of making noise, and one who had spotted a prowler. When laughter or screams drifted out of a house, he knew the sound of fun versus a cry for help. Identifying a person in pain was a piece of cake. He'd heard that distinctive timbre in Beth's voice tonight.

He'd hurt her. Deeply. Maybe so badly she'd never be willing to give him another chance.

''So you gave up your dream of setting the world on fire after all,'' Beth said over the hum of the engine. ''When you decided to come back to Newellton, why didn't you open up a law practice here?''

"Law's a funny business. Somehow everybody loses track of getting to the truth. Guilt or innocence, right and wrong, don't seem to matter much. Success is measured in how clever you can be. It went against the grain." He turned right back onto Main Street. The businesses were all dark now, the sidewalks and street empty. "At least as a cop I can try to nab the guilty ones and keep off the backs of those who are innocent."

"An honest Injun who cannot speak with forked tongue?" she teased.

He gave her an appraising look out of the corner of his eye. "Knock it off, Ms. White-Eyes, or I'll haul you in for loitering in a residential area."

"With you," she pointed out.

"Minor detail. You'll still need a smart lawyer to keep you off the rock pile."

"I think I know one," she replied softly.

Damn. Just being near Beth and hearing the sweetness of her voice sent his libido into overdrive. He hadn't ever reacted to any woman with quite the same intensity as he responded to Beth. Truth was, right this minute, he wanted to take her out to Lovers' Gulch himself.

No. That wasn't quite right. He was older now than the last time they'd gone there to neck, and hopefully a lot wiser. When he made love with Beth Haggerty—and he sure as hell wanted to—he'd like it to be in comfort. Not in the cramped front seat of an old, battered truck, or the sheriff's car.

In a king-size bed, he decided. Plenty of room to move around. Or maybe the tepee he'd raised on his twenty acres as sort of a getaway summer home. Now *that* was a place where they could have some privacy.

But he had a whole lot of fences to mend before that could happen. He needed to reestablish the intimacy they had once shared.

"At least you achieved your dream," he said. "As an illustrator, I mean."

"Sort of. I do like my work—even Winifred Wipe-Up was fun in its way—but what I'd really like to do..." She hesitated.

"Go on."

"I got a chance last year to illustrate a children's book. I'd met the publisher at one of those awful parties where you're crammed elbow-to-elbow in a tiny apartment and are supposed to pretend you're having a wonderful time." An impish grin curled her lips, and a stab of jealousy jolted Hawk at the thought some other man might have seen her smile in just that same way.

"Anyway, I talked the guy into giving me a chance. I had to work the project in around all of my advertising jobs, which meant I didn't get much sleep for a while. But it was wonderful. I could let my imagination run wild."

"What was the story about?"

"Kids on a teeter-totter. That sounds strange but it was really a supplemental science book for primary grades—levers and fulcrums, that sort of stuff. The idea was to not let the kids know they were learning anything." She shrugged. "If I could find a way to support myself doing children's book illustrations I'd consider that head and shoulders above dancing-paper-towel jobs."

He laughed. "Somehow I bet you'll find a way. My guess is that you're even more determined to prove yourself than I ever was." She was one strong lady.

Always had been. He respected that. It made him want her all the more.

Beth leaned back against the headrest. "I hate to sound like a party poop, Hawk, but my body is still on New York time. It's been a long day." Stressful, too, she thought, with all the memories of the past coming at her from every side.

And Hawk. His nearness. The fact that he had once cared. The knowledge that things could have been different. But weren't. And there was no going back.

He parked in the driveway of her grandmother's house. Before he had a chance to turn off the ignition, she hopped out of the car.

"Thanks for the dinner," she said more brightly than she would have thought possible, given the wrenching sensation she felt in her chest.

He wasn't going to leave it at that. Before she could get up onto the porch and slip the key into the lock, Hawk was there with her, turning her into his arms.

"Nobody's that tired," he said, his voice like warm velvet across her skin.

"Hawk, I really don't think—"

"For old times, Beth." His palms framed her face, holding her in a gentle vise. His head lowered toward hers. She trembled. Her hands splayed across his broad chest, pressing him away without conviction.

She could fight a lot of things—a whole town, if need be—but she couldn't fight the warmth of Hawk's lips. Not on her forehead where he brushed the first kiss. Or by her ear where his breath heated her sensitive flesh. In spite of her best intentions, she lifted her head to accept the inevitable next step.

Never could she resist the achingly familiar taste of his lips. She knew their shape and soft, moist texture.

His sweet gentleness, his eagerness. Her heart responded on its own with a heavy beat against her ribs. Her fingers clutched at the cotton fabric of his shirt.

Send him away, an inner voice urged. *You're no good for him. You'll be hurt, too. Again.* But the sound was like a poor connection on a long-distance phone call. She was here. With Hawk. In his arms. And she didn't want to listen. Not as he deepened the kiss.

A hundred heartbeats later, Hawk raised his head. His breath came in short, ragged gasps.

Beth swayed. Some small sense of reason returned. Not much, but enough so she managed a breathless whisper. "This isn't a good—"

He silenced her by pressing one finger to her softly swollen lips. "Get some rest. I'll call you tomorrow."

She started to protest again. A wise woman would. But he was gone.

As the police car pulled out of the driveway, she noticed a curtain shift in the upstairs window across the street.

"Oh, Hawk..." she sighed. Everyone in town was going to know about their kiss. If she saw him again, even once, he'd have a reputation to live down just like hers. That wouldn't be good for a cop. Not in a town like Newellton.

Shivering, she clasped her elbows and pulled her arms tight against her body. Tears threatened. She wouldn't let that happen to Hawk.

For the next three days the memory of Hawk's kiss, and her resolve not to see him again, taunted Beth. So she worked as hard sorting her grandmother's things as she could to keep busy. Ignored the phone when it rang. Which was often. And she jogged.

Running, at least, was a real joy. She'd forgotten how pleasant the open spaces and rolling hills of the prairie could be. Jogging in New York City, under the best of circumstances, meant crowds and car fumes. Here she inhaled the rich scent of the earth, as she passed freshly plowed fields, and heard the morning call of a magpie. A couple of times she'd managed to catch sight of a fox returning from his evening's hunt.

As she crested a gentle rise, Beth spotted Tommy Russell's blue pickup truck parked off to the side of the road beneath a cluster of plum trees. Two heads, one of them with a perky ponytail, were visible through the back window.

Beth smiled and shrugged. She wasn't about to tell anyone those two kids were cutting classes. That was decidedly their own business, though she didn't necessarily approve, of course. Both of them seemed intelligent enough to figure out their futures on their own. Besides, she owed Tommy her silence. He'd done a really good job on Grandma's lawn and had even taken the initiative to cut back some of the fading flowers in the garden.

Reversing her path, Beth headed for home. She wiped a drizzle of sweat from her forehead. Tommy and Annie Mae didn't need her company just now. This was not the time to discuss decorations for the upcoming dance, though Beth already had a couple of theme ideas that might be fun.

A few hours later she'd loaded Grandma Claire's old Rambler with bags of clothes and personal items to take to the county seat where there was a Heart Association thrift shop. It seemed right to give some of

Grandma's things to help support a group that fought heart attacks, the cause of Claire's death. She'd talk to them, too, about picking up the used furniture once she was ready to leave.

The trip would also provide Beth with a diversion. She was a mental wreck waiting for the phone to ring and knowing she didn't dare answer it.

Taking a road that avoided downtown Newellton, Beth had to slow as a soccer ball bounced out into the street from a local practice field. Smiling, she waited for the young boy to retrieve the ball and throw it back into play.

When she glanced at the field, her breath hitched. Hawk. Wearing shorts and a T-shirt, he ran beside another boy, shouting instructions as the kid tried to dribble past an opponent.

"You've got two feet, Danny. Use 'em both," he ordered. "'Atta boy. Now go left. Fake right! Now go for it!"

The youngster scored easily, and Hawk held up a fist in salute, then slapped the boy on the back.

Beth had to look away. Hawk coaching a soccer team was simply another sign of his commitment to Newellton, a reminder of his decision to lay down roots in the one place where she wouldn't ever feel welcome.

She felt unbidden moisture gather on her lashes and quickly drove away. Tears wouldn't do any good.

Beth knocked three times at the alley entrance to the thrift shop before someone responded.

"Land's sake! I'm coming. I'm coming." The woman who opened the door had hair the color of snow-clad mountains, lines etching her face like a topographical map of the Rockies and a very large parrot perched on her shoulder.

Beth's stomach clenched. "Mrs. Russell?"

"Ahoy! Man overboard," the bird squawked.

"Hush now, Charlie, it's just little Beth Haggerty from across the street. How are you, dear? I've been meaning to come thank you for hiring Tommy to help out around your place but I've been feeling a bit under the weather lately." She peered over the top of half glasses. "Old age, you know. Can't seem to do as much as I used to."

Except look out the window and mind other people's business, Beth thought, not a little unkindly. "I didn't expect to find you here." Or a bird.

"How 'bout tonight, sweetheart?"

Millie tapped the parrot's beak with a single admonishing finger. "Oh, I've been volunteering at this thrift shop a couple a days a week since I don't know when. Since before my dear Arnold passed on, I think. It's filled with treasures, you know." A twinkle in her gray eyes, she opened the door wider. "Come on in, child. Browse around all you like."

"No, that's not why..." Though she hated the thought of the gossipy neighbor pawing through Grandma Claire's possessions, Beth resisted the urge to get back in her car and drive on home. "I've brought some of Grandmother's things. To contribute. There're some clothes in the car. And jewelry. Just costume pieces. Nothing special."

"Aren't you a sweet thing," the older woman crooned. "Every little bit helps, you know. Let me get my cart. We'll just bring it all in and see what we've got."

"Hey, good-lookin'—"

Beth stifled a laugh.

It took four trips with the grocery cart to empty the trunk and back seat of Beth's car. Grandma Claire's clothing joined the general clutter of the thrift shop where every inch of space was crammed with used merchandise. On shelves lining the wall, porcelain figurines vied for space with toasters and children's games. One whole wall was filled with clocks of every shape and size imaginable, each one telling a different time. Racks of dresses, blouses, shirts, pants, coats and suits for all ages and sizes jammed the center of the room so tightly it was hard to find a safe passage through the maze. A musty odor competed with Millie's fresher lavender scent.

Millie draped an armload of Claire's dresses over a bulging cardboard carton. "We just got in a lovely little music box you should take a look at as long as you're here. Harriet Thurgood dropped it by yesterday." She edged past another stack of merchandise and retrieved a wooden box from the shelf. "Harriet and her husband, God rest him, bought this while they were on a trip to South America in '85. Or maybe it was '86. I can't keep it straight. Anyway, the carving is so nice—"

"I'm really not interested, Mrs. Russell. I'll just get the rest of the things from the car."

"Reef your sails, bucko." The bird flapped its wings and did a quick jumping step on Millie's shoulder.

A wall clock chimed loudly, although it read eight minutes to the hour.

Shaking her head, Beth headed for the back door.

When she returned with the next armload, Millie said, "Now I've found it. This is just the right treasure for a young girl like you." She held up a white wedding gown carefully packaged in plastic, and Beth felt heat color her cheeks. "Rachel Derrington's granddaughter wore this. Isn't it lovely? And the wedding was so nice. She has two little girls now, I think, or maybe it's a boy and a girl. I do lose track—"

"I'm really not in the market for a wedding gown. Thanks."

"A girl just never knows," Millie said, burrowing into another stack of "treasures" to find something else for Beth's reluctant consideration.

Finally, when all of the new merchandise was piled in a single heap to be sorted, Millie bustled behind the sales counter. She moved quite agilely, given her age. "Let me see. I know I put my receipt book here somewhere." She searched through the pockets of her blue shop jacket.

"It's all right. I don't need a receipt," Beth insisted.

"Yes, you do, dear. Taxes, you know. You might as well take a write-off when you can. No need to give Uncle Sam more than his due, is what my dear Arnold always said." She shuffled through a stack of papers on the counter and several colored pens and pencils fell to the floor.

Impatiently Beth picked them up and placed them back on the counter. The receipt really wasn't that important, and she had grown weary of hearing about cousin Matilda's great-aunt who had donated a whole tea set, which she had, in turn, inherited from a great-grandparent in Minnesota. No bit of historical trivia about any of her treasures seemed to have escaped Millie's notice.

"Mercy sakes," Millie complained. "I've been so busy trying to make up a poster I just haven't had a chance to—" Her head snapped up. As she looked at Beth, the old woman's wrinkled face broke into a wide grin. "Now why didn't I think of that before? You're just the person we need."

"Keel haul Polly." The bird's screech was positively ear piercing.

Beth winced. "I beg your pardon?"

"It's the white elephant auction we're having next month."

"Auction?" Beth didn't have the vaguest idea what Millie was talking about. She wasn't going to be around next month.

"I've been trying all morning to make up some fliers and a poster or two to put in store windows around town." She laughed a funny, high-pitched cackle that was surprisingly infectious and sounded amazingly like a parrot having a good time. "For the life of me, I can't seem to draw an elephant, white or any color at all."

"I don't see—"

"Dear Claire used to brag on you all the time, child. Showed me all those pretty pictures you made in school. Real creative, she said you were. Claimed it was an inherited talent, though she couldn't draw a stick figure herself that I knew about." Millie transferred the bird from her shoulder to a nearby perch.

"Land ho!"

"Well, yes, but—"

"It would take me a month of Sundays to come up with a poster that was halfway decent. But you—" Millie retrieved several sheets of poster board from behind the counter and handed Beth an amateurishly hand-drawn flier with the date, time and place of the auction scrawled across the bottom. "You just take this on home with you and when you're done, bring it on across the street. The association will be so tickled."

Beth had always thought of herself as a reasonably assertive person. She was able to tell people no politely and firmly. But not Millie Russell. That lady was like a steam roller.

Even as she drove back to Newellton, Beth wondered just how she'd agreed to draw a half dozen posters for the Heart Association in the next few days.

She chuckled to herself. Elephants weren't all that hard to do. She'd already imagined a cute character with a floppy, broad-brimmed hat, a big red heart stuck right in the middle of her chest and a parrot perched on her rump. The project wouldn't take too much time away from the clean-up job, she rationalized.

Arms and hands full of poster board and felt-tipped pens, Beth elbowed open the screen door to the house. To her surprise, the front door stood slightly ajar.

Anxiety prickled the short hairs on the back of Beth's neck.

She'd locked the door when she'd left for the county seat. She was sure of it. A New Yorker didn't forget that kind of detail, however safe and bucolic Newellton might seem.

Drawing a deep breath, she shoved the door open all the way and cautiously stepped inside.

The art supplies slipped from her grasp and clattered onto the floor.

Bile rose in her throat.

Chapter Four

"Stay here on the porch," Hawk ordered.

"There's no one inside."

"You don't know that, Beth, and neither do I." He unholstered his gun.

Her throat constricted. "I'm sorry I had to call you. I used a neighbor's phone because it made me sick to see—" She pressed her hand to her stomach. "Millie Russell wasn't home. I didn't know what else to do."

"You did the right thing." Grim lines bracketed his finely chiseled lips. "Now, stay right here."

Holding his weapon upright, he pulled open the screen door.

"Wait." She reached for him, then withdrew her hand. "Be careful."

He gave her a quick wink. "No sweat. I'll be right back."

As he went into the house, Beth sent up a zillion prayers for his safety. Fear knotted her stomach.

Dear God, why would anyone vandalize her grandmother's house? Did someone want her out of town so badly? Neither she nor her grandmother had ever hurt a soul in Newellton.

She waited for what seemed like an eternity, her nerves as frayed as the ends of an old paintbrush. Except for a dog barking, well down the street, the neighborhood was quiet. Deathly so. She strained to hear what was going on inside the house. Hugging herself against the shiver that ran down her spine, Beth fought off another wave of panic. *Be careful, Hawk.*

His sudden reappearance startled her, and she almost flew into his arms in relief.

"It's all clear," he announced.

"Thank goodness."

"You're going to have to tell me if anything is missing."

Following his lead, she entered the house. The living room was strewn with pillows and cushions, some of them ripped open and their innards spilling out onto the floor. The old encyclopedias she'd studied as a child had been tossed about in total disregard for their value, if only sentimental.

Worse was the message scrawled across the mirror above the couch. One side of her brain revolted at the words—Get Out of Town, Slut—while the other side registered the odd shade of persimmon lipstick the vandals had used.

"Why do they hate me?" The question scraped past the lump in her throat.

Hawk looped his arm around her shoulders and pulled her close against his lean, hard body. "Don't take it personally. It's probably kids . . . I don't know who all. But it doesn't mean anything."

Beth thought it did. Hadn't the town always hated her and her sister?

"They left most of the rest of the house alone," he said. "Let's take a look around to see if anything is missing."

"I haven't lived here in so long, I don't really know what Grandma—" Her gaze slid to the top of the bookcase. She swallowed hard. "The TV is gone. And the VCR." A few years before, Beth had sent the VCR as a Christmas present, knowing her grandmother loved movies but rarely had a chance to see one. In every letter Claire had extolled the merits of some new video....

Beth blinked away the sting of tears at the back of her eyes. She felt as if the memory of her grandmother had been violated along with her home.

"I don't suppose you know the model or serial numbers," Hawk asked.

"Maybe I can find the warranties. Grandma kept files on everything she owned."

"That would help."

Together they toured the house. In the kitchen, glass shards covered the floor in a pointless show of wanton destruction, and the microwave was missing.

"Odd," Hawk mused. He kicked some glass out from under his boot. "They took stuff that's easy to sell or hock, just like the other break-ins we've had in town . . . but the vandalism is different."

"Including the cute little message they left?" she asked, not even trying to hide the bitterness she felt.

He slanted her a glance. The expression in his dark eyes caressed her softly. Dear God. Why was she taking her anger out on him?

"I'm sorry about that," he said. "If I catch whoever did this..."

For a dozen heartbeats he held her gaze. A warm sense of being protected and nurtured curled through her body. She hadn't felt that way in a very long time. Certainly not while living alone in her New York apartment.

Abruptly she turned away. She couldn't let Hawk start to care for her again. Nor did she dare admit her feelings were still so near the surface.

"I'd like to check upstairs," she said. *I'd like to get out of Newellton with my heart intact.*

For a moment she considered simply hiring someone to clean out the house, then she'd take the next plane back to— But that didn't make sense.

She hadn't expected to come across Hawk again. Even returning home she'd had no reason to believe he was still here... or that she would react so strongly to him. She'd been only a kid when they were together. Didn't maturity change how you felt about your teenage crush? she wondered.

Not when you really love someone. As hard as she tried, she couldn't ignore the insistent response that came from somewhere deep in her heart.

Hawk followed her up the stairs, checking on each room off the hall, most of which had been left untouched by the vandals.

He knew immediately which bedroom belonged to Beth. It was awash with bright colors, as vibrant as a sunrise and very much like the woman herself. Reds, golds and pinks, with splashes of green, a shocking blend that immediately lifted his spirits. He hated that she looked so dejected now, and cursed the crooks who had taken the sparkle from her eyes.

"Subdued isn't exactly your style," he observed dryly.

"Color is meant to be enjoyed. Otherwise we would have all been born color-blind like cats."

"Interesting thought." The room was more than a reflection of Beth—the gold of her hair, the green of her eyes and the vitality of her personality. He caught the scent of her perfume still hovering in the air. An electrifying combination. "Maybe you'd like to help decorate my house when I get it built."

She hesitated. "I won't be here, Hawk," she reminded him softly.

"Yeah. I keep forgetting." He jammed his fingertips in his hip pockets. Damn! There had to be some way to get her to reconsider Newellton. The vandalism sure as hell hadn't helped.

He let his gaze slide around the room. A smile quirked his lips.

"You kept the eagle feathers I gave you," he said.

A bit of color tinged her cheeks. "You dubbed me Little-Brave-with-Big-Stick. How could I throw them away? I certainly wouldn't have wanted to offend your Crow ancestors."

"I'm sure they appreciate your concern." He hoped maybe there was another, more personal reason she'd kept his small gift.

She lifted the three feathers down from their prominent place on the wall. "Maybe I should give these back to you now. So you can return them to your people. After all, in New York—"

"No." He curled his fingers around her outstretched hand. Though her bones were delicate, she had a strength that couldn't be denied. "Keep them for whatever protection they can bring you." So you won't forget me.

The tips of the feathers trembled slightly.

"There's a certain amount of irony, that I had to come back to Newellton to get burglarized, don't you think?" she asked. "The city is supposed to be more dangerous than a small town like this."

"It is. Usually." He took the feathers from her hand and placed them carefully on the desk next to the window. He should have given her more than a few feathers all those years ago but he'd been flat broke. A guy on a scholarship who waited tables to make ends meet didn't have much spare change to spend on gifts for his girl.

His eyes caught a sketch pad leaning against the wall. "Yours?" he asked, lifting it from behind the desk. "You never showed me any of your drawings."

"I was just a kid then. I wasn't very good." She tried to pull the pad from his grasp.

"Good enough to get into the most prestigious art school in the country. You must have had some talent."

"Really, Hawk, I don't want you to see—"

Hawk flipped to the first page. A sharp thrill of pleasure ripped through him. The charcoal sketch was unquestionably of him mounted on an Indian pony. He was bare from the waist up and in his hand he carried a spear. Eagle feathers dangled from his coiled hair.

"I'll be darned . . ."

"I told you they weren't very good."

"You lied." He turned one page after the other. The drawings were superbly done, each one featuring him in a dramatic and very traditional Indian pose. "Didn't I ever wear any clothes around you?"

She giggled, but the sound was more embarrassed than amused. "Those probably reflect an overdose of adolescent hormones on my part."

He recalled his own level of testosterone had been sky-high when he was hanging around with Beth. It still was. What worried him now was the way she had once imagined him.

He closed the cover on the sketch pad. "You know, that really isn't me, Beth. There's more to me than simply being an Indian."

"Of course. I know that. Artistic license."

With his fingertips, he lifted her chin. For a moment he studied the wild curls of her hair, the few light freckles across her nose, the depth of her eyes. Then his gaze settled on her lips. Desire tightened in his gut.

"I've never in my life gone on a buffalo hunt, Beth. I respect and honor my ancestry, and maybe it helps me appreciate the land a little more fully, but I'm just as at home in a twenty-story building or working a computer spread sheet. I'd like you to see me as a man of both worlds."

Beth swallowed hard. "I do." She was also acutely aware they were standing in her bedroom, the late-afternoon sun slanting through the window curtains. The light cast Hawk in a bronze glow that made her ache to paint him again, to catch on paper the shifting shadows across his strikingly handsome cheekbones so she'd never forget them.

His seeing her old sketches was like having him read her diary. She'd poured her love into each stroke of charcoal or pen. When she drew the breadth of his chest, it had been as though she was actually feeling the texture of his flesh, his warmth and his corded muscles rippling to her touch. She had taken hours getting the shape of his lips just right, knowing how they would feel on hers. Every sun-burnished crinkle at the corners of his eyes had been lovingly drawn.

She shouldn't be thinking about any of that. Hawk shouldn't have pried.

"You are a very good artist," he insisted.

"You're just saying that because of my model." She tried for a tentative smile.

"No. I can't draw a square box myself, but I took a couple of art appreciation classes. I really got into it. Visited a lot of galleries. Hung out at the museums."

"When we were dating you never said anything about liking art."

"I guess I'd never given it a try. Then I heard you won a high school award. Figured I ought to broaden my experience."

Because of her? She felt a bubble of pleasure rise inside her and immediately she tried to suppress it.

"Sometimes when I went to a gallery," he continued, "I'd see a painting that triggered a memory. Then I'd just sit there and think about you."

Her heart thudded a heavy beat.

Just as she'd thought so much about him? Not that it had done either of them any good.

"Isn't it time to get on with the investigation?" she asked, forcing herself not to dwell on what she'd really like to have happen here in her bedroom. "Check for fingerprints or something?"

He rasped his thumb across her lower lip and she trembled. "I've got the fingerprint kit in the car. I'll get it."

When he left the room, she expelled the breath she hadn't known she'd been holding. Her knees felt weak.

Still clinging to the sketch pad, she sat down heavily on the edge of the bed. *Grandma Claire, what am I going to do?*

There was no way she could stay in Newellton. Hawk didn't seem to understand that. Yet her heart was screaming there'd never be another man like him. Not for her. And if she weakened her resolve, it would only hurt Hawk and leave her with memories she'd never forget.

Better to hitch her star to Winifred Wipe-up than lose her heart again, she thought with a sigh.

A few minutes later she heard male voices from downstairs. Shoving the sketch pad to the far back of the closet and pulling her fragile emotions together, Beth went to investigate.

She stifled a groan. Everybody's favorite mayor was on the scene. She had the distinct feeling Taylor Franklin was like an oversize bird of prey anxious to pick her bones clean. He must have heard about the break-in on the police radio, she concluded.

"We've got to find out who's doing all this breaking in, Hawk," the mayor insisted.

"I'm trying, Your Honor." Hawk blew a charcoal powder across the top of the bookcase, then rolled out a piece of clear tape.

"What is this? Sixth or seventh burglary in the last couple of months?"

"The eighth. But the M O is a little different on this one."

"That's about as big a crime wave as I can remember around here, boy. It doesn't set well that you're in charge when—"

"Just exactly what does that mean, *Your Honor?*" Hawk straightened his back and leveled the man a narrow-eyed look.

"Well, tarnation," he sputtered. "You let them damn kids from the reservation run wild in town. I know they're your people but all the same—"

"Look, neither you nor I have any reason to suspect reservation Indians are the perpetrators of this crime or any other. Instead of making unfounded accusations, you and the town council would be better advised to cut loose with enough money to hire another deputy sheriff. One lone patrol car just can't do the job." A muscle rippled his jaw. "Even I'm allowed to sleep sometimes."

The mayor's puffy cheeks turned such a bright red, Beth thought he might have a stroke. Hawk didn't notice. He'd already returned to his work. She wanted to cheer him on for letting the mayor have "what for" but she kept her lips zipped. No sense in angering the man any further.

Turning his head, Franklin nailed Beth with a snide look.

"Maybe the problem is you've been doin' too much *sleeping,* Hawk, since Miss Haggerty came back to town."

She saw Hawk's hand close into a fist. Before he had a chance to do something stupid—like hit his de facto employer, Beth stepped between them.

"I appreciate your concern about the break-in, Mr. Franklin. Nice of you to drop by." Do let me hurry you on your way. Before Hawk flattens you, *and* loses his job.

"For all we know, missy, this whole mess could've been your own doing."

"Are you saying I vandalized my own house?" Her blood pressure rose by several degrees. One more remark like that and she'd blow a cork before Hawk did.

"People do that sort of thing, you know. People without morals. For the insurance money."

"Oh, sure," she fumed. "Like I'm going to file a claim for a ten-year-old television set I was going to give the Heart Association anyway."

"It's possible." He lifted his chubby chin and looked down his nose at her. "Other members of your family have been known to lie. I'm sure our deputy sheriff will remember to—"

"Maybe you're behind all this. You're the one who wants me out of town." She thumbed over her shoulder at the message on the mirror. "Just what shade of lipstick does your wife wear, Your Honor?"

"Now see here, young woman. I won't tolerate—"

"That's enough, Franklin." Hawk's warning snaked out like a whip.

Beth took an angry step forward. "Stay out of this, Hawk," she ordered. "He's talking about my sister! I won't let anyone—"

"Calm down, Beth." Gripping her shoulders from behind, Hawk restrained her. "I think you'd better leave, Franklin. I'll let you know the results of my investigation."

"You do that, boy. You just do that little thing." He straightened and buttoned his jacket over his rotund stomach, stretching the fabric to its limit. Like a pompous, balding Buddha, he left the house.

Beth thought she might burst.

"You've got to watch your temper, Beth. It doesn't do any good to—"

"*My* temper? What about yours?"

"He made me angry. I'll admit that. But keeping calm—"

"You were going to hit him, Hawk. I saw your fist." She jabbed her finger into his chest. "Why do you think I said one word to the creep? Because I was afraid you'd cream him and end up in the unemployment line. Or arrested for assault and battery. That's why!"

"You actually started that argument to protect me?" His eyes widened in surprise.

"Of course I did. You would have jumped right in there if I hadn't, just like you did when I was a kid. Admittedly things got a bit out of hand—he's such a sneaky fighter—but I'd just as soon never talk to the man. And wouldn't have except for you."

A rumble started low in his chest, crept upward until Hawk leaned back his head, giving full rein to his laughter. The sound was warm and wonderful, begging for company.

Beth resisted even while the corners of her lips twitched. "Hawk, Taylor Franklin isn't a laughing matter."

"No, but we're quite a pair." Tears glistened at the corners of his eyes. "We were so busy *protecting* each other, we're both likely to get run out of town on the next freight train."

"You were protecting me?" A giggle threatened.

"Of course, Little-Brave-with-Big-Stick. I figured if I didn't stop the argument, the next thing I knew, I'd be arresting you for scratching his eyes out."

"He just makes me so mad I wanted to—" She'd wanted to prick his flab with a hat pin to see if he'd go flat. Stick ice picks in his car tires. Graffiti his house. *Damn.* Newellton, in particular Taylor Franklin, always brought out the absolute worst in her. When was she ever going to grow up? Or simply not care about people like the mayor anymore?

Hawk pulled her up hard against his chest and wrapped his arms around her. She inhaled his musky, masculine scent. His hand slipped through her hair, and she felt his breath flutter the strands away from her face. In spite of the total futility of the idea, what she really wanted was to have Hawk make love to her and forget the rest of the world. But she couldn't do that.

"I think I'd better get this place cleaned up," she whispered, though there was no conviction in her voice.

For a time his only reaction was the heavy beating of his heart against her cheek and the achy, throbbing response she felt much lower in her body.

"Yeah. I gotta get my work done, too." The husky timbre of his voice vibrated down her spine.

Good sense warred with her desire to stay within the circle of his embrace and won.

She was still sweeping up broken glass when he appeared at the kitchen door, metal fingerprint kit in his hand.

"I'm all finished," he announced.

"Find anything?"

"Lots of partials. I suspect they're all going to be yours. Whoever did this was careful. Wiped the door clean."

"How'd they get in?"

"Probably slipped a credit card through the lock. Your grandmother really should have had a dead bolt."

"There's never been any reason in this town."

"There is now." He shifted the weight of the box in his hand. "I gotta get this back to the office and make some calls."

"Sure."

"I hate to leave you alone."

"I'm all right," she lied. The burglary had made her feel both violated and vulnerable. Meanwhile, her level of frustration was going off the chart. She gritted her teeth.

"You'll lock the door?"

"Of course. But you just said it wouldn't do much good."

"I'll come by to check on you as often as I can."

Don't. That isn't wise for either of us. "I'll be fine."

"Worrying is my job."

She smiled. "You do it very well."

Later that night as she was getting ready for bed, she glanced out the window. Hawk's car was parked across the street. The poor man wasn't going to get any rest at all.

With a sigh she realized she'd rather have him inside. At least she felt safe enough with him watching over her to get a good night's sleep.

Maybe tomorrow she'd find time to work on Millie's Heart Association posters. Clearly she needed a distraction.

Outside, Hawk pulled up his jacket collar. The nights were getting damn cold. Winter was going to show up any day.

There wasn't any real reason for him to park in front of Beth's house. Until now, at least, the burglars hadn't hit the same victim twice. Not much point when they'd just been cleaned out. Still, the added vandalism troubled him.

He'd always found sitting at a stake-out was a good time to think. Right now he wanted to come up with a couple of dozen reasons Beth would want to stay in Newellton. There were already two strikes against his plan—Taylor Franklin and the break-in. He hated starting anything from in a hole.

As the light went off in her bedroom, Hawk decided he'd simply have to redouble his efforts.

Chapter Five

"Yoo-hoo! Hello, dear!"

Beth cringed inwardly. She couldn't even take out the trash without Millie Russell spotting her.

Forcing a smile, she greeted her neighbor and eyed the parrot sitting on the woman's shoulder. What an odd pair.

"I just wanted to thank you for the posters, dear. The elephants are adorable." She tittered a high-pitched laugh. "Whoever heard of an elephant with reading glasses?"

"It was a fun project." It had been enjoyable, as well as a diverting way to keep her thoughts off of Hawk. She had, however, left the artwork on Millie's front porch in an effort to avoid a scene just like this.

"I must say Charlie's delighted to be included. He preened over his picture for hours."

"I'm glad he's pleased." Do parrots experience emotions? she wondered. She hefted the black trash

bag onto the heap that was already sitting by the curb.
A late-afternoon breeze fluttered the pages of an old
magazine she'd discarded on top of the stack of papers.

Millie turned to her parrot. "Tell her thank you,
Charlie."

"Wanna come up to my place, babe?"

"Babe?" She choked on the word. "Mrs. Russell,
wherever did you get that bird?"

"Oh, land's sake. My son did this to me. He caught
me talking to myself one day—you know, after my
Arnold passed on—and said I'd be better off talking
to a bird." With the back of her finger she stroked
Charlie's yellow beak. "I guess my boy thought I'd
end up on the loony farm if I had to quit talking al-
together."

Entirely possible. "His vocabulary is...a bit unusual." Definitely rated PG-13.

"Shocking, isn't it?" The old woman's eyes twin-
kled. "Puts one in mind of pirates and such. I've always suspected my son got Charlie on sale at half price
without hearing him speak a single word. Serves him
right for trying to save money on a present for his
mother."

"Hi-ya, toots!"

A laugh tickled the back of Beth's throat. To cover
her amusement, she brushed a streak of dirt off of her
jeans.

"I taught him that one myself." Millie lifted her
chin like a proud parent whose child had just gotten an
A on his report card. "I always secretly wanted someone to call me 'toots.'"

It was impossible not to smile. Mrs. Russell certainly had a way of growing on a person.

"I really do have to go," Beth said. "I've only worked my way through half the rooms and there's still—"

"Oh, I'm sorry, dear. I know I ramble on. Can't even blame that on old age. My Arnold used to say I was the talkiest woman this side of Chicago." With a smile, she offered a plateful of homemade muffins. Beth had been so fascinated with Charlie, she hadn't noticed the woman was carrying anything. "And here I almost forgot why I came across the street in the first place. These are for you, dear."

"You didn't have to do that." The scent of warm apples and cinnamon teased at Beth's nose.

"Of course I didn't. But I like to cook almost as much as I like to talk, and it's just no fun to cook for one."

Beth tended to agree, not that she was given a chance to express her views.

"I'm always bakin' up something for the grand-children. They think that's what grandmas are for. Now their parents, well they worry all the time about sugar and such, but as I see it—"

"Thank you, Mrs. Russell. I'm sure I'll enjoy the muffins."

"I made enough for you and that young sheriff, if he comes by. Nice boy. He surely has been worried about you since your break-in."

Heat crept up Beth's neck. The only time the Neighborhood Watch had fallen down on the job was when she'd needed it as protection against vandals. Hawk had shown up at her house every day since the burglary, each time with a new excuse. No doubt the whole of Newellton was fully aware of his comings and goings. Probably to the second.

She let out a sigh. Some things you just couldn't fight. She was beginning to think both Millie Russell and Hawk fitted into that category.

"My goodness," Millie said. "Here comes the deputy sheriff now. Must be hoping for a dinner invitation tonight."

As Beth turned to watch the Jeep coming down the street, she felt her heart do a fluttery quickstep. She wondered if she would ever get over the tingle of excitement that kept her on edge when Hawk was around. Probably not. Not as long as she stayed in Newellton.

"Come on, Charlie. These young folks don't need us meddling old fools around."

The bird dipped his head. *"Reef your sails, Bucko."*

Millie, talking nonstop to the parrot, scurried back across the street, the hem of her print dress blowing in the breeze.

Beth was still laughing when Hawk pulled into her driveway and got out of the car.

"You look happy." He tipped his hat rakishly to the back of his head, smiling in a way that brought crinkles to the corners of his eyes. Lord, he looked good in his uniform. It fit across his broad chest as if it had been hand tailored.

"It's Millie Russell and her bird." And seeing Hawk, she thought, reluctantly admitting she'd been anticipating his visit since morning. "I swear she knows everybody's business in town." Most especially mine.

"Every town needs someone like Millie."

"How do you figure that?"

"It's like an oral history—the same thing as the storytellers among my people. If they didn't pass on the folklore, it would be gone forever and our lives would be less rich because of it. Every culture needs a Millie."

"I have the feeling Newellton has more storytellers...I'd call them gossips...per capita than any other town on earth."

"Maybe that makes us better off." He gave her a one-sided grin that started the fluttery feeling in her chest again. "What have you got there?" he asked.

She pulled the plastic wrap off the muffins. "Millie said she made enough for both of us. She thinks you're staying for dinner."

Selecting one from the plate, he took a big bite. "Hmmm. Good. Am I?"

"Are you what?"

"Staying for dinner."

"Oh." A little crumb stuck at the corner of his mouth. She watched as he licked it off, cursing herself for wishing she could have done that. A tight little thrill raced through her just at the thought. "Depends on what your excuse is today for dropping by."

"Excuse?" he asked innocently.

"First it was that little girl..."

"Iona?"

"Right. Iona desperately needed help to create a medieval castle out of cardboard for a class assignment and I was the only person in the whole county who could help."

He grinned. "She got an A."

"I should hope so. It took us half the night." There'd been glue spread all over the kitchen by the time they were done, and the three of them had laughed so hard it was a wonder the castle hadn't collapsed. As it was, the poor thing had come out with a lopsided tower.

"Then yesterday you came by with all these certificates of appreciation to be calligraphied."

"The Boy Scouts are going to have their awards banquet." She watched another bite of muffin go into his mouth.

"And in between you sent Annie Mae and her friends over to see me about the dance decorations."

"You help 'em out?"

"We came up with a theme they thought would work. It will take them a few days to get everything together, but it ought to be a big hit."

"I knew you could do it." He looked quite smug.

"So, Deputy Sheriff Raymond Hawk. What's your excuse today?"

"Well, I . . . I was up most of the night because of a three-car crash on the highway. I didn't have time to think of one." He didn't in the least look contrite. "Can I stay for dinner, anyway?"

She laughed. What else could she do? She certainly wasn't keeping any secrets from Millie Russell. Besides, she'd bought chicken breasts at the market that morning—just in case.

"Come on in," she said. "You'll get your dinner, but this time I'm going to put *you* to work."

"How's that?"

"I've been cleaning out cupboards like crazy. Unfortunately, I filled the boxes so full I can't budge them. What I need is a man with a strong back and not too many brains—"

"Now wait a minute," he objected with a grin, following her up onto the porch. "I've got all of these degrees—"

"Won't do you any good tonight, fella. Trust me. In this case the only things that count are muscles. Big ones."

The slow grin curving Hawk's inviting mouth and the sudden arch of his left brow sent a tingling sensation clear down to Beth's toes. To avoid acting on a determined impulse to kiss him, Beth turned her back and headed for the kitchen. She simply had to stop thinking like that.

Hawk discovered Beth had not spoken in jest. He'd practically strained his gut on more than one of those damn boxes. He wasn't complaining, though. In fact, under other circumstances he would have been happy to help her with whatever she needed done. But he didn't want to help her leave Newellton forever. And that's exactly what was still on her mind.

He'd been trying to get her so involved in the town she wouldn't have time to think about New York. Clearly his plan wasn't working.

After he washed up, he went in search of Beth. His nose told him something good was cooking. When he found the dining room table set for two, candles included, a smile curled his lips. A romantic atmosphere? Maybe he was making some progress after all.

Beth pushed out through the kitchen door carrying two plates. "Hope you don't mind eating in the dining room."

"Not at all." Too bad Grandma Claire didn't have a stereo. A little mood music would be nice.

"I've always loved this rosewood table. I figured this might be the last time I'll get to use it. A guy from an antique store is coming out next week to take a look and make me an offer on it."

Hawk's hopes deflated like a car tire running over a row of "Danger—Don't Back Up" spikes. "It won't fit in your apartment?"

"Not a chance." She reached for her chair and he pulled it out for her. "Thank you, kind sir. My apartment's so small I'd have to get rid of every other stick of furniture I own to keep this, not that much of my stuff is worth keeping."

"If the table's important to you..."

"I keep thinking someday I'll be able to save enough, and earn enough, so I can have a real loft apartment. Something really special where the lighting would be just right for my painting. Then I'd have enough space for a dining area. But that dream's a long way off."

Hawk took a bite of chicken covered in a light apricot sauce. It tasted fine but he suddenly didn't have much of an appetite. "I understand the light's real good right here in Montana."

Her fork paused in midair. "Yes, I suppose it is. As a matter of fact, I sketched Millie's posters on grandma's back porch. It's north-facing and glassed in. I'd almost forgotten... I used to do a lot of painting out there...." Memories washed over her—some bad, but mostly good, particularly those of the long, lazy days she'd spent engrossed in her artwork. Winter days with the snow blowing across the landscape. Summer when afternoon clouds spilled out over the plains and heat waves shimmered up from asphalt streets.

The big Montana sky. Nothing in New York could compare with that.

Darn Hawk for reminding her. She knew exactly what he was up to, and it wasn't going to do any good. She couldn't stay in Newellton.

She clamped her teeth down hard on a bite of chicken that had suddenly turned to cardboard. The baked potato didn't taste much better.

"Any luck locating Grandma's TV set?" she asked, intentionally changing the subject. She simply wouldn't think about "what-might-have-beens."

"No sign of it yet." He shook his head thoughtfully, contemplating a piece of zucchini dusted with little bits of seasoning. "I've sent out bulletins in the ten western states trying to track down all of the stolen goods we've lost in the last couple of months. Notified pawn shops, local police. So far I've come up empty."

"So where'd it all go?"

"My guess is that whoever is doing this has stashed the goods somewhere—probably nearby. Then when they're ready, they'll haul it off all at once. Maybe as far as California to a swap meet."

"Makes it hard to track."

"Almost impossible." He yawned and mumbled, "Sorry about that. Late night."

"Must have been a bad accident."

"Hmm. Three cars, four injuries. A couple of them pretty serious, plus two fatalities."

She hadn't realized he dealt with problems much beyond the city limits. "Do you always have to respond to accidents? I mean, isn't that what the Highway Patrol is for?"

"Depends on where it is and how bad. In this case, one of the drivers evidently fell asleep. He crossed the divider head-on into the westbound lane. It wasn't pretty." A haunted look wavered in his eyes.

Her heart went out to him. "If you were up half the night, you must be tired. I shouldn't have worked you so hard."

"I'm okay. I caught a catnap this morning." Head bent, he studied his plate. "Sometimes it can get to you, though. One of the victims was a five-year-old kid. Thrown clear out of the car. He never had a chance."

In an instinctive gesture, Beth placed her hand on his forearm. He'd rolled up his sleeves, baring flesh that was warm and smooth and very tempting. "I'm sorry, Hawk." She wanted to do more, to take him in her arms and accept for herself some of the pain he was obviously feeling. Who did he usually turn to for comfort? she wondered, wishing it could be her.

He shrugged and forced a weak imitation of his usual cocky smile. "It's the kind of thing you just have to put behind you. Thanks for the sympathy."

"Anytime." For the next week or so.

"You got a deal." Visibly relaxing, he leaned back in his chair. "Say, you remember when we used to play Scrabble at this table with your grandmother? I think she was trying to keep us from spending too much time alone together."

Her grandmother's efforts at chaperoning hadn't been entirely successful, as Beth recalled. She and Hawk had always found a few moments for a quick kiss. She wondered if Grandma Claire knew what they'd been doing in the kitchen when they were supposed to be fixing popcorn. Probably, she thought with a tender smile. "Sure I remember. You beat the socks off me every time we played." She'd done better at the kitchen games.

Forking the last of his chicken into his mouth, he said, "Yeah. You weren't very good."

She "humphed" at him. "So spelling wasn't my forte. Bet I could take you on now."

"Think so?" He cocked a curious eyebrow. "You take a remedial Scrabble course at that art school of yours?"

"Not exactly." Finished with her meal, she placed her fork and knife across the plate. "When I was doing all that hiding out at the library, I found a book called *Scrabble Made Fun,* or something like that. I learned every trick there is." At the time she'd hoped Hawk would come back and she'd be able to show him how much she'd learned. But she'd never had the chance.

"That, Ms. Haggerty, sounds very much like a challenge to me."

"Now?"

"Sure. Why not?"

"Well, I . . ."

He shoved back from the table. "You know where the game is? I'll give you a twenty-point handicap."

"Don't get overconfident, Hawk. I've got zygote, zoysia, and xylan right at my fingertips."

"Xylan?"

"Would you believe quoin, quip, quasar and quaff?"

"Maybe I'd better make that ten points."

Smugly she added, "Pyx, pyre and pyknic, with a y."

"That's not a word."

"Sure it is. I'll prove it . . . if I can find the dictionary."

"All right. All right." Laughing, he threw up his hands in mock surrender. His dark eyes sparkled. "I'll play you even."

"Count your blessings I didn't take advantage of you when I had the chance."

They cleaned up the dinner dishes together, laughing and coming up with outlandish words—most of them of their own invention—they intended to use to beat the other. Then Beth went to retrieve the Scrabble game from a give-away box Hawk had already taken to the garage. When she returned, she found him stretched out on the couch . . . sound asleep.

"Oh, Hawk," she sighed. Quietly she placed the game on the coffee table.

He looked exhausted. With his mouth slightly open, he snored lightly. Not enough to disturb a person, it was almost a reassuring sound. Very masculine. Strangely comforting. And frustrating as all get out.

She brought down a blanket from upstairs to cover him. Millie Russell would have to reach her own conclusions about why Hawk's car was parked in the driveway all night. For herself, Beth simply didn't have the heart to wake him.

For a long time she sat in a chair watching him, observing the subtle movement of his chest, the shape of his tapered fingers, the distinctive arch of his eyebrows. From time to time he shifted his position in his sleep, giving her a new feature to admire. The straight line of his nose, the flair of his nostrils. His sensuous mouth.

His long, dark hair was particularly intriguing. Thick. As midnight-black as a raven's wing that caught the reflection of the table lamp and invited a woman to run her fingers through its richness.

She blew out a sigh.

She must be a masochist, she decided. Just looking at Hawk and knowing they'd never be together was like flaying herself raw with a thousand whips. Yet she couldn't stop herself. It was as though she needed to absorb his every nuance so there'd be no chance she could forget any line, shade or angle. The memory would have to last her such a very long time.

Eventually she went upstairs to bed, though she didn't fall asleep very quickly.

Her next awareness was of the smell of bacon and Hawk's rumbling voice saying, "Rise and shine, sweetheart. Breakfast."

She pried one eye open.

Hawk grinned down at her. "That's my girl."

She groaned. "Oh, God. You're a morning person. It's barely light."

"Best time of the day."

Pulling the blanket up over her head, she mumbled, "I hate people who are cheerful before noon."

He lifted the covers and peered at her. "You're a morning grouch?"

Lord, he looked good. "I'm not grouchy. I simply don't talk this early in the morning."

He sat down on the edge of the bed. "What do you do in the mornings?"

"I get up very slowly, do my stretching exercises, and then, when there's time and the weather's decent, I go for a jog."

"But you don't talk."

"No."

"You're talking to me."

"That's because I'm incredibly polite." She was also aware Hawk was sitting dangerously close to her, his hand resting very near a particularly intimate part of her anatomy. That's what she would describe as a real wake-up call. A heated one, at that. "I also don't eat breakfast. Only coffee."

"That's bad for you."

What was bad were the images that kept skittering through her mind. Hawk. Her. Naked. Entwined together on her bed.

She pulled the sheet back over her head. "If you'll get out of here, I'll try to get my act together."

"No breakfast in bed?"

That was positively the last thing on her mind. "I'll join you downstairs in a minute."

His low rumble of his laughter filled the room, doing a number on her pulse rate. Darn him. He knew exactly what she was thinking. *Join* hadn't been a wise word selection at all.

When she finally heard Hawk leave the room and the door close behind him, Beth uttered a sailor's curse that would have turned Charlie's beak red. She had to get over this persistent fantasy that had gripped her since she'd returned to Newellton. He was just a guy, she told herself resolutely, knowing it was a lie but unwilling to acknowledge her true feelings even in her heart. It simply wouldn't do any good.

She dressed quickly in jeans and a T-shirt. Heaven forbid Hawk would come back upstairs to see what was taking her so long and catch her in an even more vulnerable circumstance than in her bed.

She hurried downstairs.

Humming softly to himself in a kitchen filled with the scent of bacon, eggs, toast and fresh-perked coffee, Hawk created a very domestic scene. Wouldn't it be something to wake up to that every morning? Beth thought with an internal groan. It would certainly get a woman's day off on the right foot.

Her stomach growled.

"You see?" he said, handing her a cup of steaming coffee. "You are hungry."

"Coffee's fine. Thanks." His cocky grin was doing enough damage to the quivery feeling in her midsection. Adding food might prove disastrous.

"I kept your eggs warm."

"Later." Maybe she could handle them for lunch.

As she drank her coffee, Hawk straddled a chair and continued to eat his breakfast. She watched him consume every single bite. Someone really ought to tell him about cholesterol. He needed a caretaker. Too bad she couldn't be the one.

"Are you going to be able to talk sometime soon?" he asked cheerfully.

"Is there a rush?"

"I thought I'd apologize for falling asleep last night."

"I knew you were faking. You didn't want to risk me beating you at Scrabble."

"Not so." He chuckled a warm, low sound, and Beth wrapped her fingers more tightly around the coffee cup. "As soon as you're able to function, I'd like to take you to see my place."

Chapter Six

"Your place?" she echoed. His room over the beauty shop?

"My land. It's about five miles out of town. I'd like you to take a look at my house plans. Maybe give me some decorating ideas."

That sounded a whole lot like being invited up to look at some guy's etchings. Not a good plan.

"Hawk, I still have tons of work to do around here. I'm already way behind schedule. Thanks mostly to you and your assorted projects. I can't go running off—"

"It won't take long. Couple of hours, max. Then I'll help you with whatever you want. I've got the whole day." He shoved aside his breakfast plate.

Beth had the distinct feeling she'd traded the mischievous imp on her shoulder for a tempting devil in the form of Deputy Sheriff Hawk. His seductive voice and his dark eyes crinkling at the corners were both very persuasive.

Darn it all, she wanted to see where he was going to live. She wanted to be able to picture him striding across his land when she was sweltering in a New York summer. She was definitely a glutton for punishment.

''The storm windows have to be put up,'' she objected lamely, watching for his reaction.

His triumphant smile skated along her nerve endings. She felt like a rainbow trout that had just been lured by a very tasty bait . . . hooked, but good.

Hawk extended his hand across the table, sealing the bargain. ''It just so happens putting up storm windows is one of my all-time favorite things to do.'' He was about to play very nearly his last card. If seeing his property and plans for his house didn't tempt her to linger in Newellton, then he didn't know what would.

''You lie,'' she accused but accepted his hand.

He ran his thumb slowly along her knuckles. ''A sworn officer of the law . . . lie? Not a chance.''

''I hope you never have to testify in court. There it's called perjury, and they lock you up and throw away the key.''

The corners of her lips twitched into a smile, and the golden specks in her green eyes sparkled. She was fully awake now. And very desirable, as she had been all curled up in her bed. To his great delight he'd discovered she slept in a sheer nightie that left little to the imagination. It had taken all of Hawk's willpower not to shed his clothes and slip under the covers with her. He would have made swift work of that wispy bit of nylon.

''I'll keep that advice in mind, Counselor.''

''See that you do.'' She pulled her hand free of his.

Immediately he missed the feel of her delicate bones and her supple flesh warm against his. He sure as hell hoped this plan would work better than his others had.

As they cruised out of town in the Jeep, Beth noticed Tommy Russell's truck parked beneath the same stand of wild plum trees where she'd seen the teenager and his girlfriend before. Young love, she thought with a twinge of envy.

"I ought to give those kids a hard time," Hawk grumbled, seeing the truck, too.

"Leave them alone," she urged. "You're only young once." And can never go back, however much you might like to.

"It's a school day."

"Somebody make you the truant officer?"

He threw her a sideways look. "I hate to see kids mess up. That's all."

"You'll just embarrass them if you stop now. Maybe you can mention something to Annie Mae... quietly...when you're at the café." She hated it when anybody got nosy about somebody else's business. Live and let live. That's the lesson she'd learned from the Gossiping Gerdies of Newellton.

He shrugged and glanced into the rearview mirror as they went past the spot where Tommy had parked.

A mile further on, Hawk tapped his siren and pulled over a couple of cars filled with Indians from the reservation.

"What's wrong?" she asked. "Were they speeding?"

"Not that I know of. I just want to talk."

As he got out of the car, Beth tried to tell herself it was Hawk's job to keep track of what was going on in the community. Still, it didn't sit quite right. She sure wouldn't want some cop looking over her shoulder all the time. Myrtle Symington poking her nose into Beth's business had been bad enough.

She watched Hawk saunter toward the men. They were relatively young, maybe late teens and early twenties. They greeted Hawk as an old friend with handshakes and slaps on the back.

Beth couldn't hear what was being said, but she noted a different way Hawk carried himself. Taller. Straighter. With considerable authority. And the men responded with deference. For some reason she felt like an invisible observer at a meeting of the braves from his village. Not one of the men glanced in her direction. It made her feel oddly uncomfortable.

When Hawk returned to the car, she asked, "What was that all about?"

"Just some guys I know. Sometimes they hear things I don't."

"Like what?"

"Who's been flashing some extra money around lately. Rumors. Kids who've gotten a burr under their saddle. Somebody who needs some bucks in a hurry." He pulled the Jeep back onto the road and tossed a salute to the men still standing beside their cars.

"Were you asking about the break-ins?"

"Yes. I thought they might give me a lead."

Hawk hadn't been idly passing the time of day, she realized. He was really doing his job. "Then you think Taylor Franklin is right? It could be kids from the reservation?"

He slanted her a glance. "I didn't say that. Fact is, I'm absolutely stymied. And they weren't much help.

Did say they'd keep their ears to the ground for me, though.''

Hawk lived in two worlds, she mused, just as he'd tried to explain to her. He seemed quite at home in either or both. The woman he eventually chose for himself would be hard-pressed to manage the same balancing act.

"You know," she said thoughtfully, "if they'd only taken the TV and stuff I wouldn't have minded so much. After all, I was going to give it away. It was that message on the mirror that really got to me."

"I know. Something doesn't feel right at all. And I don't like puzzles that have missing pieces."

As he wheeled the vehicle off the narrow highway onto the rutted track to his land, Beth gazed across the landscape. Beautiful did not begin to describe the rolling grassland that led down to a creek lined with cottonwood trees. Though the grass had turned brown with the approach of winter, and the wild array of sunflowers and milkweed had long since turned to seed, she could imagine the glory of color they had offered during the summer. Her heart lodged in her throat. She ached to find her drawing pad, to sketch the seasons as they marched across his land.

In spring, purple lupine would wave among the newly green grass. Along the creek there'd be the soft tumbling sound of water running over the rocks and the whimpering chatter of newborn porcupines. She'd never see or hear any of that. Because she would be gone. She mourned the loss as surely as an artist would cry out in anguish against the threat of going blind.

Dear God, help me to be strong, she prayed. Though she might want it otherwise, she didn't belong anywhere near Newellton.

He stopped the Jeep and turned toward her. "What do you think?"

"Lovely." The word formed thickly in her throat.

"There've been some complaints from environmentalists about the big ranchers breaking up their lands into smaller chunks, but I figure I'm darn lucky to own twenty acres."

"No neighbors." It was so quiet she could hear a woodpecker tapping its beat down by the creek.

"The closest place is just over the rise. You can just make out the path." He leaned across her to point, and she caught a tempting whiff of his musky masculine scent. "It's owned by Irene Whitefeather. She runs the alcohol rehab center at the county seat and has a couple of the cutest kids you'd ever want to meet."

"Some place to borrow a cup of sugar."

"She makes a heck of a good cup of coffee, too."

That sounded like Hawk and his neighbor had shared more than one.

"Come on," he said. "Let me show you around."

Holding her hand, he led her to the highest point of land and stood proudly looking around him. The sound of the breeze teasing the dry grass whispered in the air. Far off in the distance a tractor hummed; closer at hand a magpie called.

"The middle of the creek is the western border," he said, "so I have water rights." With a sweep of his free hand, he pointed north. "From the road to the tips of those trees you can just see is all mine. Not bad for a kid from the reservation."

She squeezed his hand, dittoing the same feeling of tightness that constricted her heart. "Very impressive."

Flashing her a confident grin, he said, "Next on the tour is my tepee. My aunts made it for me. All very authentic, including the absence of electricity and running water."

"How 'bout a sweat house?"

"I've been thinking about putting in a sauna when I build the house. Would that do?" They scrambled down the knoll.

"You're the one who's supposed to know whether the Indian spirits would approve."

"I'll have to check."

He'd located the tepee in a sheltered spot not far from the creek where it was shaded by cottonwood trees from the afternoon sun. The structure was bigger than Beth had expected, a dramatic addition to the landscape, while at the same time it seemed to fit. She could easily imagine Hawk's ancestors camped here by the water and could almost hear the sounds of a village at work and play.

He lifted the flap for her to enter.

For a moment their eyes met and held, his dark and seductive, hers more hesitant. Her heart beat heavily against her ribs, her breathing irregular. If she went inside, into the intimacy of his tepee, she might well come out a different woman. But if she refused his invitation, there would be a part of Hawk, the way he lived, she would never know and couldn't hold in her memories.

Steadying herself, she ducked through the opening.

Mellow light. A pleasant scent of cold ashes and animal skins. The trappings of a man visiting his roots—a bow and arrow, water skins, leather containers for his personal items and a heap of furs piled thickly for a bed.

Hawk's hand warmed the small of her back. "Welcome to my summer home."

"It's a very...peaceful place." In spite of the riotous feelings threatening her midsection and accelerating her pulse.

"Pull up a seat on the bed. I'll get the house plans."

Her gaze slid to the pile of pelts. Hawk's bed. Where he slept and dreamed and where she would like to—

The furs accepted her weight like a soft, sensuous pillow. She plowed her fingers through the strands, imagining how the fibers would feel against her bare flesh. Beads of perspiration formed across her forehead.

"Here we go." Hawk sat down beside her and rolled out the blueprints. His thigh brushed against Beth's, and she fought a groan of frustration that rose in her throat. She clenched her teeth.

"I told the architect I wanted something that would fit into the landscape. Nothing gaudy or too big."

"It's perfect," she agreed, noting how the house was designed to nestle against a knoll as part of the land, not a showy add-on. Meanwhile she struggled valiantly to ignore his closeness, his primitive scent, the strong shape of his hands and the smooth muscles of forearms she wanted to touch. Those same arms had the ability to hold her tight, to make her forget what it was like to grow up a "Haggerty girl," with all of the awful reputation to overcome.

"When I was a kid," he said, "we always lived in places that were hardly more than shanties. I hated it. The dirt and squalor. Cars and rusty old junk filling up the yard. Half the time the plumbing didn't work, assuming we had any. I promised myself..."

Beth heard both pride and vulnerability in his voice. She'd known he'd been poor but hadn't realized just how much it had bothered him. His determination had driven him all the way to law school, she realized, and his roots had brought him back home again. "Looks like you're going to make your dream come true." She wished she could do the same with hers, too.

"Yeah. Close enough, away." He grinned. "The plans call for two bedrooms now, and later I can add on a new wing with another bedroom and an office. Just in case."

"In case?"

"I figure to marry someday. Have kids. Makes sense to plan ahead."

"Of course." Her stomach muscles clenched. She didn't know if it was from jealousy because some other woman would bear his children or the result of an even more basic desire.

"You'll like this." He pointed to the north-facing side of the house. "That's supposed to be kind of a family room but it would be easy to put in a lot of glass and some skylights. Perfect for a studio."

She licked her lips. She didn't want to talk now. Not about studios or lighting or anything else. She wanted . . .

"Hawk?" The sound was little more than a whisper.

He turned, his expression questioning. Then his eyes darkened with understanding of her unspoken plea.

The blueprint forgotten, his hand palmed the column of her neck, his thumb rasping along her jaw. His eyes were dark and hooded. Without a word, he slowly lowered his head to hers.

The hunger of his kiss rocked Beth. A responding urge uncoiled deep within her, making her feel that she was on the verge of some great discovery, one she'd dreamed about all of her life. She savored his flavor, as fresh as creek water flowing free and wild in spring. The current pulled her onward, eroding her resistance.

Reaching to his nape, she untied the thong that held his long hair in place. The rich strands settled across his shoulders and brushed against her cheek, making her feel as unfettered as he. Wild. A part of the land.

Heated sensations swept over her; her heart beat almost painfully. She was acutely aware of his masculine scent, the breadth of his shoulders and the softness of his bed beneath her. Every spot where their bodies touched became a pleasure point of building desire.

"Hawk." She mouthed his name against his lips. "I have the feeling you brought me here to seduce me."

His lips shifted into a smile beneath hers. "The thought did cross my mind."

"I'd always hoped . . . I wanted you to be the first."

Expertly Hawk stretched her out on top of the soft furs. "It doesn't matter how many others there've been. Today . . . us . . . is all that counts." This was the moment he'd been waiting for. He had to show her how much he cared, how good they'd be together. There'd never been another woman who had become so much the center of his life. Her past didn't matter. Only now.

"There hasn't ever been anyone else." The whisper of her words brushed warmly against his face.

He paused, grooves tightening his forehead. "You've never..." Hope and surprise surged. "You're still a virgin?"

Beth tensed. Something in his incredulous tone made her wary—or maybe it was her own insecurities and residual common sense. If anyone else in Newellton had thought she'd been with a thousand men, she wouldn't have cared. The same question coming from Hawk hurt. Deeply. Had he always wondered if she was like her sister Marilee?

The fact was she'd never wanted anyone else. Not even once. Now he doubted her.

She braced her hands on his chest. "Did you assume I've had dozens of lovers?"

"Well, no, I didn't mean that. But you're a beautiful woman. After all these years living in the city. Hell, I didn't expect—"

"It's all right, Hawk." Fighting the sudden urge to cry, she squirmed away from him. "We shouldn't be doing this, anyway. I've got my return trip ticket to New York all bought and paid for. We don't need to complicate our lives." *I don't need to leave something of myself here in your tepee that I'd never get back.*

"Beth, hold on a minute." He reached for her but she eluded his grasp. The center of her breastbone ached with disappointment, making drawing a breath nearly impossible.

She slipped out of the tepee, blinking at the bright sunlight. To her surprise she saw a dark-haired little boy running toward her down the path from the neighbors.

"Hawk! Hawk! Mom needs you," the child cried.

Chapter Seven

Hawk appeared at the entrance to the tepee. He flicked Beth a puzzled look, then shifted his attention to the child. "What is it, Nick?"

"It's Bengie. He got outta his pen 'n' he's rootin' around in Mom's vegetable garden. She whacked him a whole mess of times but he won't go. She said she seen your car." The nine-year-old finally took a breath. "Can you come?"

Hawk hesitated a fractional beat. No question, he and Beth needed to talk. He didn't understand what had gone wrong. What he'd said shouldn't have upset her so much. Lord, would *men* ever understand women? It *had* been ten years and admittedly he hadn't been celibate all that time. He wasn't about to lay some double standard on her.

Besides, he'd been so pleased he would be her first lover that he could hardly remember what he'd said.

"What's a Bengie?" Beth asked in a flat voice. Her arms were folded across her waist and her face was a colorless mask.

Damn. He'd hurt her and he didn't know how or why. "Bengie's a monster hog that Irene owns. On the loose he can do a heck of a lot of damage."

"Then you'd better help your neighbor."

"Will you come with us?"

Her gaze slid from his to the Jeep and back again. He could almost hear her considering a long walk home.

"I suppose."

He breathed a sigh of relief. They'd talk later. "Okay, kid, lead the way. We'll see if we can corral Bengie before he eats up all your winter stores."

Beth followed Hawk and the boy along the path, while they trotted far ahead of her. Her legs felt heavy. She shouldn't have visited Hawk's tepee. From the beginning she'd known it was risky business. She simply hadn't realized the treacherous gamble she'd taken with her own vulnerabilities. She'd slipped into a trap of her own making.

She loved Hawk. Try as she might, there was no way she could continue to deny it. She'd even been ready to physically express her feelings, all the time knowing they had no future together.

Foolish woman. Where would that have left her?

And the question in his eyes, the doubt that she had waited all this time for the one man she could love had been like a knife twisting through her heart.

With the back of her hand, she swiped away the tears that threatened. She'd be damned if she'd let Hawk know just how much she'd been hurt.

When she crested the ridge she discovered bedlam.

A reluctant smile tugged at the corners of her lips. Hawk was in full pursuit of the biggest pig she'd ever seen. The creature lumbered steps ahead of him, moving far more agilely than she could have imagined possible. The animal grunted and squealed. Hawk swore. Loudly and often, in a couple of different languages.

Off to the side, a woman clearly of Indian descent was bent over double she was laughing so hard. Her hand rested on her son's shoulder and a much younger girl clung to her legs. The vegetable garden, or what was left of it, looked like it had been plowed by a maniac. This year's turnip crop had definitely seen better times.

From a corral well away from the action, two pinto ponies looked on with considerable disdain.

Hawk dived for the pig, missed him by inches and landed spread-eagle in the dirt. He came up sputtering.

"Watch out, Beth! He's comin' your way."

Good grief! She was about to be trampled by a thousand pounds of— "What do I do?"

"Herd him to his pen."

Herd? Is that what Hawk had been doing?

Knowing she couldn't outrun the animal, she knelt, as much in the hope the pig wouldn't be able to focus on her, as anything else, and crooned softly, "Hi there, piggy. My, aren't you a beautiful boy. Would you like me to paint your picture?"

The pig slowed.

"Yes, I know that mean ol' man has been chasing you, but he's just trying to help." They were now eye-to-eye, and Beth wondered anxiously if pigs could bite. Gingerly she reached out to pat his snout. "Why don't

I take you back where you belong? Would you like that?''

She stood. The pig nuzzled up against her thigh.

"Come on, sweetheart. Let's show Big-Chief-Toma-Hawk how it's done."

As though he were on a leash, Bengie trotted along beside her. She led him through a gap in the split-rail fence of his pen. Continuing on to the other side, she hopped over the fence.

Turning, she smiled smugly at Hawk, who was covered with dirt and mud, a few vegetable stalks dangling around his shoulders.

"How did you do that?" he asked, panting.

She lifted her chin. "I have talents you haven't yet begun to plumb."

He mumbled an unpleasant sound she couldn't quite decipher, and she choked back a laugh.

"I'll get the fence back together," he said aloud.

The Indian woman approached her, an amused smile softening her distinctive features. "You must have spent a lot of time around pigs to get Bengie to behave like that," she said. "Thanks for your help."

"That's about as close to a hog as I'd ever want to get. I was raised in town."

A flash of recognition appeared in the woman's dark eyes. "You must be Beth Haggerty." She extended her hand. "I'm Irene Whitefeather."

Resentment clawed at Beth. Had her reputation as a hellion extended to the local Indian tribe?

"Nice to meet you." She forced a polite smile as they shook hands.

"Hawk's been so excited you were back in town."

Beth raised a questioning eyebrow.

"Oh, my...I hope...I mean, I'd seen Hawk's car go by. He's never brought anybody to see his place that I know of. I just assumed he was alone...." The color on the woman's cheeks deepened. "I hope sending Nickie over didn't, well—"

"He was just showing me his land and house plans. I'm going back to New York next week."

"Oh." She finger combed her daughter's dark hair. The child looked to be about three. "This is Margo. Hawk's been really good for her. She doesn't understand why her daddy isn't around anymore, and he's kind of taken up the slack."

"I see," Beth replied tautly.

"My husband died about a year ago. An accident. He was a truck driver."

"I'm sorry."

The woman eyed her curiously. "Hawk and I have known each other for a long time. We're friends. Nothing more than that."

"I didn't ask."

"No, but you were sure thinkin'." Irene laughed.

This time Beth was the one who blushed. The woman was very perceptive. "I'm sorry," she repeated, feeling foolish.

"Don't be. He's a hunk. There're a lot of women around town who'd like to get their hooks into him, but I'm not one of them. We're way too much alike." She placed a caring arm around Beth's shoulders. "Come on. For getting Bengie back in his pen, the least I can do is offer you a cup of coffee."

Irene's immaculately kept house was far more modest than Hawk had planned for himself. Beth wondered how the woman could work full-time, keep up with the house, and still have energy to spend with her children. The kids were adorable, just as Hawk had said.

He stood leaning against the kitchen counter, his booted feet crossed at the ankle, sipping his coffee. Beth had selected a ladder-back chair at the table.

"The darn licensing bureau is giving me fits again, Hawk," Irene said, stirring sugar into her coffee.

"How's that?"

"The rehab center. They claim, after all these years, the zoning's wrong." Little Margo gave up her grip on her mother's leg and switched her attention to Hawk.

Picking her up, he placed her next to him on the counter and tweaked her nose. The child giggled. "It's a little late for that kind of complaint."

"Tell me about it," Irene agreed. "The problem is politics, as usual."

"Maybe you should get the mayor to help you out," Hawk suggested. He tousled Nick's hair as the boy got a glass of milk from the refrigerator and got a one-of-the-guys smile in return.

"Actually, Franklin serves on our board of directors. He has a problem with tunnel vision—" Irene shrugged and laughed softly "—but in this case he has been talking to the county people. If we're going to get past the bureaucrats, he may be the key."

Politics made for strange bedfellows, Beth mused. That Taylor Franklin would be useful for anything was a surprise to her.

She listened to the ebb and flow of the conversation without being able to contribute much. She knew virtually nothing about alcoholism or Indian affairs and suddenly felt like something was lacking in her education.

Watching the youngsters interact with Hawk, their youthful eyes so dark and intent, Beth was struck by how much she'd like to have his children. She wanted to see his cocky grin on the face of their son, his ebony eyes sparkling with humor reflected in the same eyes of their daughter. The feeling burrowed under her skin and knotted painfully in her stomach. She could never have any of that. She simply didn't belong. Not in Newellton and not among the members of his tribe.

Irene, or someone like her, would be a much better wife for Hawk. The realization hurt.

Gathering her willpower together, she said, "Hawk, I still have a lot of work to do at the house."

"Yeah. Sure." He'd washed up as best he could but there were still streaks of dirt across his shirt. Somehow that small mar in his perfection made him all the more appealing. "Storm windows, coming up."

He lifted the child from the counter to the floor, and Beth said her goodbye to Irene. In some other time and place, they could have been friends. She liked the woman's openness, the way she offered friendship with no strings attached, in spite of her obvious questions about Beth's relationship with Hawk.

Not that any true relationship existed beyond Beth's fantasies.

As they walked back toward the Jeep, Hawk slipped his arm around her waist. Beth felt a little piece of herself die at the sweet possessiveness of the gesture.

"How 'bout we go back to the tepee," he suggested, his voice suddenly filled with husky undertones that arrowed into Beth's midsection. "Seems to me we left some very important business unfinished."

Beth stepped out of his reach and kept on walking. "No, thanks. The only business I'm interested in is getting out of town."

In two strides he had blocked her path. "Beth, we've got to talk."

"There's really no point." She tried to step around him but failed.

Reaching into his pocket, he pulled out the car keys. For a moment he dangled them in front of her and then folded his fist around them. "We're not going anywhere till we get this settled. I know I upset you but I'll be damned if I know how. Talk to me, Beth. We were so close—"

"That's what you wanted, isn't it?" she challenged. "To be *real* close."

"You did, too, Beth. You can't deny that."

No, she couldn't, but she wasn't about to admit it. Aware that he knew just how much she'd wanted him made her feel excruciatingly vulnerable. "You expected me to put out just like every other guy in Newellton has expected it since I was thirteen years old. After all, I'm a Haggerty girl."

"You know that's not what I think."

"Isn't it?" She set her lips into a grim line. "I saw that look in your eye when I stupidly announced I'm still a virgin." Hell, it wasn't a crime. In fact, more than once she'd tried to get that interested in a guy. It hadn't worked. Every time, when things had heated up, she'd thought about Hawk.

She started to leave but he stopped her, whirling her around by the shoulders to face him. He was so close she could feel his breath hot across her cheeks.

"I don't know what you think you saw but I'll tell you what I was feeling. So pleased I wasn't sure I'd be

able to control myself, or go slow enough so it would
be good for you. I didn't want to hurt you. Sure I was
surprised. Maybe that was in my eyes, too. But dammit all, I never thought I'd be that lucky.''

"You ... you didn't think I was lying about—"

"Not for a second."

His words rolled across the quiet of the grasslands
like the pealing of a church bell. An invitation she
didn't dare accept.

"Thank you for believing me," she said softly.

His hand slid to the column of her neck. "Always."

"Truth is, I've always run kinda scared from this
sex business. Because of what happened to Marilee, I
think." And because the torch I carried for you simply wouldn't burn out.

"It's nothing to be afraid of. Not where we're concerned."

That was exactly why she shouldn't make love with
Hawk. She didn't dare leave that much of herself in
Newellton.

"You believed me once today. I appreciate that.
Now you've got to trust me about this, too, Hawk.
We're not right for each other."

Pain shadowed his dark eyes. "How can you be so
sure?"

"Same song, old verse. I don't belong in Newellton. You do."

"You could try."

"It wouldn't do any good. Too many memories.
Mine and everybody else's. The hurts run too deep."
She covered his hand with hers, cherishing the feel of

his long fingers, the masculine texture of his skin. "That's what happened in the tepee, Hawk. Because of who I am, all of those doubts came back. I guess what I was reading in your eyes were my own fears and insecurities."

"It doesn't have to be like that. You could give the town, and me, a chance."

A sigh escaped her lips. "Let's get the storm windows up."

With a shake of his head, he helped her into the Jeep.

Afraid she might turn into a pillar of salt, she resisted the urge to look over her shoulder for one last glance of Hawk's land. She would remember it, anyway. Every tree and blade of grass. And the way, for just a few moments, he had held her in his arms.

Back in town Beth waited in the car, while Hawk went up to his room to change clothes. Having nearly made love with him in the tepee, she certainly didn't want to risk more intimacy in the close confines of his bachelor apartment.

Besides, it looked like half the old ladies in town had beauty appointments in the shop downstairs. They were sure getting an eyeful of Beth sitting out front.

Though she intentionally looked in the opposite direction, it didn't stop Myrtle Symington from pausing beside the Jeep.

"Are you getting arrested?" the woman asked.

Gritting her teeth, Beth bit back an unpleasant response. "Just waiting."

"Well, I hadn't heard you'd done anything wrong...yet."

She gave the nosy old woman a plastic smile. "If I do, I'm sure you'll be among the first to know."

"I suppose." Myrtle shrugged and headed back to the grocery store across the street, her hairdo in perfect order.

Beth fumed. She felt like crawling under the dashboard, but she wasn't about to give the townspeople the satisfaction of knowing they'd forced her into hiding. It was bad enough Marilee had felt compelled to run away. For the moment, Beth decided, Newellton was stuck with her.

A few minutes later Hawk appeared and drove them back to Grandma Claire's house, to Beth's great relief. She hated to be the object of so many unfriendly stares. If she didn't feel entirely at home in New York, at least she was ignored.

"Hey!" Beth complained. "You're supposed to be squirting the windows with that hose. Not me!"

"Sorry 'bout that."

"I bet." The wicked gleam in Hawk's eye suggested he was anything but apologetic. "This isn't a wet T-shirt contest, you know."

He gave her one of those looks that had her heart knocking against her rib cage. "Maybe I should talk to the town council. Seems to me we could find some sponsors."

"Oh, swell." With a rag, she swiped at the glass on the storm window. "Then I'd get blamed for leading all you men astray."

"I'm willing if you are."

She groaned. Her reputation in town was about as bad as it could get. Organizing a wet T-shirt contest would be the last nail in whatever small welcome she'd received. Not that it mattered. She'd be gone soon.

What was even more disturbing was the way Hawk looked. When they'd stopped at his apartment he'd changed into a pair of cutoff shorts. He had incredible legs, smooth, sleek and well muscled. He looked like he could be a long-distance runner or a professional soccer player.

To top it off, he'd removed his shirt on the warm autumn afternoon. Another serious distraction. Each time he lifted a window to hang it in place, his muscles rippled across his back, shifting his burnished skin in ways that made her want to run her mouth and tongue over every part of his exposed flesh. She wondered what he'd taste like. A mix of salt and sweetness, she imagined.

She gritted her teeth. Missed your chance, dummy. She grimaced, tossing aside the drying cloth after she finished wiping the last window.

"Hawk, if you've got everything under control here, I'm going to start work on Grandmother's attic. It's the last great bastion for the original pack rat."

"Sure," he responded over his shoulder. "I can handle the rest on my own."

Hawk twisted the fastener down tight. The temptation to follow Beth into the house and take up where they'd left off at the tepee was nearly overwhelming.

He muttered a curse. If he'd just kept his mouth shut, he could have had her. Once. He wasn't at all sure anymore that once would have convinced her to stay in Newellton. She seemed so damn determined to get back on that plane to New York. Stubborn woman! In fact, from what she'd said, intimacy might have sent her jetting home in a hurry. Damn!

Climbing down the ladder, he realized time was definitely running out. In just a few more days, they'd call her flight number and she'd be gone.

Balling his hands into fists, he stared at the remaining storm windows. He'd always hated this job.

The attic smelled of dust and disuse. Stacks of boxes, only a few of them labeled, filled the cramped space along with old bed frames, oak chests of drawers and oddities like Grandma Claire's wire dress mannequin. From the slender shape, Beth concluded her grandmother had had a pretty good figure during the years she'd sewn her own dresses. Age, she recalled, had added only a few inches around the older woman's waist.

With a sigh Beth opened the first box. She would try to sell the furniture to the antique dealer, but she wanted to be sure nothing personal went out the door without examining it first.

It was like working her way back through time. Her own letters to her grandmother from college were neatly arranged in one box along with some of the sketches she'd sent. Another carton revealed Beth's entire school record—report cards, notes of praise or despair from her teachers, class pictures. Marilee's history filled another container, each item lovingly retained.

Tears lodged in Beth's throat. She hadn't realized sorting through all the family memorabilia would be so difficult.

The years stretched back to her father, his years in school and his marriage to Beth's mother. Volumes of black-and-white photos.

Some items Beth set aside to take with her back to New York. There had to be some space in her apartment for her family's history.

She shoved one box out of the way and discovered a framed oil painting tucked in behind it.

Removing the dust cover, Beth stared at the familiar features of a beautiful young woman with close-cropped blond hair in the style of the thirties and a Madonna smile. Except for a drape of fabric across her thighs, the woman didn't have a single stitch of clothing on.

"Grandma Claire?" Beth whispered incredulously. "Is that really you?"

A little laugh, a mixture of pride and amazement, chortled up from her throat. It had to be a portrait of her grandmother when she'd been in her twenties. Beth had seen enough old photos to be sure of that.

But nude? The thought brought another smile to her lips.

Nobody ever thought of their *grandmother* as a nude model. No wonder the portrait had been well hidden at the back of the attic.

Beth's gaze slid to the artist's signature.

Feeling suddenly light-headed, she sat down heavily on the floor, staring at the name. "J. Ambrose," the distinctive scrawl read. Jason Ambrose was prob-

ably one of the most famous American artists of the
Depression era. She'd seen dozens of his paintings in
galleries and museums, though she'd never heard of
him painting nudes. His were usually character stud-
ies of weather-worn old people who'd struggled
against the elements on farmlands across the country.
The critics called him the one man who had truly
painted the faces of America.

And his portraits were worth a fortune.

Chapter Eight

"**H**awk! Look what I found!"

Beth burst out onto the front porch only to be halted in her tracks.

"*Fire a salvo,*" Charlie squawked, flapping his wings. "*Boarding party! Boarding party!*"

"Hush, Charlie," Mrs. Russell ordered. "What is it, Beth, dear? Did you find some wonderful treasure in Claire's attic? I've been telling everyone I know there'd be wonderful things hidden away in this house. Claire was such a saver. Never threw a thing away."

Beth shifted the painting in her hands, startled to find Millie Russell and Hawk enjoying a glass of lemonade and a plate of cookies in the shade on the porch.

"Well, I..." She really didn't want Millie to see the portrait, but it was already too late.

"Oh, my, wasn't she a pretty thing." She gazed at the painting through her half glasses. "Claire never•

said a word about..." Millie clucked like a mother hen. "My, my, my..."

The bird made a noise that sounded very much like a whistle.

Beth scowled.

Hawk eyed the portrait with interest, too. Deep grooves formed parenthetically on either side of his smiling lips. "Beautiful," he said. "I didn't realize how much you and your grandmother resembled each other."

His gaze slid from the object of their discussion to Beth. She had the very distinct feeling of being undressed...slowly. As he took her in with a lazy, indolent look, her breasts tingled and a lump formed in her throat.

Resisting the urge to cover both herself and the painting, she said, "I'd never thought about the resemblance before."

She didn't want to think about it now, at least not the part about being totally unclothed for Hawk's very masculine scrutiny. How could her grandmother even have allowed... Now that was a silly reaction. Beth had painted any number of nudes while in art school. But not so well, she admitted, or so sensuously, with brush strokes that seemed incredibly personal. Unless Ambrose had known her grandmother on more than a first-name basis, Beth would eat her membership card to the National Gallery.

"The subject of the painting is not the only interesting thing," Beth insisted, her fingers folding more tightly around the frame. "Check out the artist."

Hawk and Millie studied the signature.

"Sakes alive!" Millie sat down on the porch swing and fanned herself with a napkin. Charlie hopped off her shoulder onto the table and planted himself next to the cookies. "Is that really *Jason* Ambrose?"

"It looks like it to me." Beth cocked her head. "Do you know him?"

"Oh, my goodness, yes. I wasn't more than eighteen or nineteen then, but he was the kind of man a woman just can't forget." Her cheeks flushed, she took a long drink of lemonade. "I even saw a PBS show about him, oh, ten years or more ago, before he died. My Arnold almost turned it off, I was so a-twitter."

"Why would you be so excited about seeing a show—"

"He had the most wonderful eyes. A very bright green, as I recall, and so expressive. A little like yours, now that I think of it," Millie mused with a sigh. "He was also the smoothest talker you'd ever want to meet. My goodness, butter wouldn't melt in his mouth."

"Are you saying Ambrose was actually here in Newellton?"

"He certainly was. Came through here when times were tough, lookin' for folks to paint. They paid him a little when they could. Mostly he worked for his supper and a place to stay."

Beth poured herself a glass of lemonade. There could be Ambrose paintings in half the attics in town, she realized.

"Would he have known Grandma Claire?" she asked.

"I think the answer to that is pretty obvious," Hawk pointed out from his seat on the porch railing. He rolled the cold drinking glass between his palms.

"Now just let me think a minute. It was such a long time ago." Millie scooped Charlie back onto her shoulder and hand fed him the cookie he'd stolen from the plate.

"*Good Charlie,*" the bird crooned.

"Claire was such a nice girl," Millie continued. "So quiet and reserved like. But there was some talk..."

"Gossip about Grandma Claire and Jason Ambrose?" The gossips of Newellton had a long and not necessarily accurate history.

"Nothing ever came of it, that I can remember," Millie responded. "Jason was quite a lady-killer, as we used to say, and he sort of spread his favors around. Took a different girl to every dance. Though Claire was certainly one of them."

"Did she see him often?" Beth asked. Often enough so the guy would know her grandmother as intimately as the painting suggested?

"I don't quite recall. Things were so different then. Not many of our parents would let us have what you young folks call a date. Only a few of the boys had cars. 'Course, Jason did, him being a little older 'n' all. Made him right popular with the girls."

"Just how long was he in town?"

"From the fall harvestin' on through the winter, seems to me. He helped out all around the local farms with the hayin'. Surely did give us girls somethin' to think about on cold nights." Millie's laughter sparkled with youthful memories.

"But Grandma and this man—"

"I don't like spreading rumors. Not after all this time. But some folks said Claire was spending a whole lot of time out at the Radison place, a few miles down the highway, and that's where Jason was staying." Millie offered the plate of cookies to Hawk and he took two. "Come spring, Jason moved on. It wasn't long after, that Claire married your grandfather. A good, steady town boy.''

Propping the portrait against the wall, Beth studied the picture again. The artist's ability to communicate emotion was quite amazing, and enviable. He'd captured the same look of love in Claire's eyes that Beth had seen Annie Mae share with Tommy. An expression she desperately tried to hide when she was around Hawk.

''Then nothing ever came of their relationship, if there was one,'' Beth said.

''Well, now, I wouldn't quite say that.''

Shifting her gaze back to Millie, she asked, ''What do you mean?''

''Well, now... there's some things you just don't want to look at too carefully.''

''Millie, if you know something, you've got to tell me.''

The woman fussed with her bird, stroking his vibrant green feathers and patting his head. ''Your father, such a fine young man, was born prematurely. About six months after Claire married your grandfather. There was a whole lot of finger counting goin' on, specially since he weighed nearly nine pounds.''

With a sinking feeling, Beth registered Millie's revelation. Obviously her grandmother had had to get married because she was pregnant with—

Her grandfather's child? Or Jason Ambrose's?

In either case Grandma Claire must have suffered in the same way Marilee had when she was the victim of wagging tongues. Thank goodness Grandpa had married her.

Beth picked up a cookie. It was sinfully sweet, with double-double chocolate chips.

"Millie, did anyone think—"

"Your daddy was a rock, Beth. He worked so hard in that ol' hardware store. Knowin' Jason..." The woman shook her head. "I don't think Hank had a bit of artistic talent in him. Right down to earth, he was. Just like your grandpa."

Then where, Beth wondered, had she gotten her artistic talent? She'd never even considered the question. And why had Grandma been so terribly excited when she'd evidenced a spark of interest?

"Your talent is inborn, Beth. Use your gift, my darling," her grandmother had insisted. She'd saved every single sketch and painting Beth had created; insisted, when given the chance, that Beth *had* to attend the Art Center—for her future.

She'd known, dammit, just what genes had flowed through her granddaughter's veins. Yet she'd never told her.

And her grandmother's violent reaction to rumors that spread about Marilee? Could that, too, have been because of her own experiences? It seems the Haggerty women had always been the talk of the town.

The thought was absolutely mind-boggling.

"Beth? Are you all right?" Hawk asked. He placed his hand on her shoulder, providing a feeling of warmth against the shivers that threatened.

"I'm fine. Just...surprised."

"Now don't you go worrying about the past, dear," Millie insisted. "All of that was a long time ago, water under the bridge, you know. It's like that nice young lady Hawk brought here to visit some years back. They said you two were goin' to get married but nothin' came of that."

Beth slanted him a curious look.

"You're talking out of turn, Millie," Hawk warned tautly.

"Oh, now, isn't that just like me to let the cat out of the bag." Millie fussed with her tray of goodies. "She was a pretty thing, I'll grant you that. But mercy, so uppity. Always wearing those fancy designer suits and high heels. And fingernails so long she'd never be able to do a lick of honest work. I never thought—"

"Enough!" Firmly Hawk placed the pitcher of lemonade back on her tray. "We both appreciate the cookies you brought but I'm sure you have other—"

"Sakes alive! You're right. I really must run. The Garden Club meets tonight and I'm supposed to bring refreshments." Scooping up the tray, Millie hurried down the steps to the walkway.

"S'long, toots," the parrot squawked.

"Now you two have a good evening," Millie called over her shoulder. "And don't you worry about Claire. Dear soul, she's gone now. Nobody will fret a bit about that nice picture. Such a lovely girl..."

Shaking her head and chattering at Charlie, Millie scurried across the street.

Beth's thoughts were so scattered she could hardly sort through them. Her grandmother a nude model for the man who'd been her lover? And possibly Beth's biological grandfather? Then there was the woman Hawk had intended to marry. Millie Russell had certainly rattled her complacent acceptance of facts as she'd known them.

She dragged her gaze away from Millie's retreating figure and looked at Hawk. "Do you believe everything she just told us?"

"About your grandmother?" He lifted his shoulders noncommittally. "The evidence is pretty clear

Claire knew the artist. That doesn't necessarily prove she modeled nude for him."

"You think a painter could do a work like this in such exquisite detail just from his imagination?"

A smile tugged at the corners of his mouth. "You've got some real good sketches of me upstairs, and I don't remember posing for you. Or wearing my breechclout and feathers when you were around."

"That's different," she protested. "I was just a kid—"

"With the same kind of talent as Jason Ambrose."

His compliment took her breath away but she knew it wasn't true. "No one would put me in a class with Ambrose. Not even close. I'm just an illustrator. Winifred Wipe-Up and cute little elephants are my style. I figured I'd be darn lucky to make a living in commercial art, so I didn't even take any fine art classes."

"Maybe you should have."

He said it so simply, as though she had overlooked the most obvious fact in the world, that Beth took a step back. Had she not made full use of her God-given talents? she wondered. Gifts that had been passed on through Jason Ambrose's blood line?

It hardly seemed possible. Yet the thought, the missed potential, stunned her into rethinking her whole future.

"So what are you going to do with the painting?" Hawk asked. He was still bare-chested. An enticing drop of condensation from his lemonade glass edged down the center of his muscular chest.

Beth resisted the urge to wipe the spot of water away with her fingertip...or taste it with her lips, which was an even more tempting idea. "I don't know. The first step would be to have it authenticated, then . . ." Her mind raced. "Do you have any idea how much an Ambrose is worth?"

When she named a figure, Hawk blew out a long breath. "You'd sell your own grandmother?"

She giggled. "Not Grandma. Just the painting . . . and then only because . . . Do you realize I could buy any loft in New York City with that much money?" And maybe get serious about not only illustrating children's books but exploring a whole lot of techniques and mediums she'd never even tried.

A frown darkened his face, and his eyes narrowed. "I guess that's what you always wanted," he said gruffly, shoving his fingers into his hip pockets. "I got a couple of more windows to put up. Better get on with it before it gets dark."

"Wait a minute. I'll help you." She slid the painting inside the screen door out of sight and followed after him, his sudden change of mood quite puzzling.

As he climbed up the ladder and hefted a window into place, he asked, "Why don't you just go on back to the attic, Beth? Maybe you can find something else you can turn into cash." His voice was filled with stinging nettles.

"Hey, who pushed your button? It's not that I want to sell the painting. I'd love to be able to keep it. But I may not have that luxury." Not if I'm even considering quitting my job.

"Just like you can't keep the rosewood table you love so much." The muscles of his forearm bulging, he tightened the fastenings down so tight the new owners of the house would never be able to get the window off next spring.

"Owning an Ambrose gives a person options. That's all."

"And the only option you can think of is getting back to New York as fast as you can."

Her stomach knotted. They were back to that subject again. "I haven't noticed you trying to be flexible and volunteering to move back to the city." *Where we could be together.*

"I told you why I left."

"Did it ever occur to you there might be other legal jobs in New York you'd enjoy more than the one you had?"

"No." He turned to look down at her, his eyes very dark in the fading light. "That woman Millie Russell mentioned ... her name was Diana. She's a lawyer. Pretty damn high-powered, too. I brought her out here for a visit to see if she could handle living in a small town. I figured there'd be some good chances for her at the county seat. Government, maybe. But she would have no part of it."

"And you were determined to put down roots again in Newellton." *Pick anywhere else, Hawk. The moon, if you'd like, but not here.*

"I'd already landed the job with the sheriff's office. It's what I wanted to do."

"So you sent your lady love home to the big city to cry alone."

"I don't think that's what she did. She got married a year later to a guy who's planning to run for Congress next election. She's doing just fine, and we're still friends."

"Swell." Jealousy that Hawk had loved someone else warred with the empty feeling that settled in her midsection. To think she'd nearly made love with him that morning, and now the utter futility of that dream was once again apparent. A stick of dynamite wouldn't blast the man out of Newellton.

Hawk hung around long enough for dinner and a quick game of Scrabble. She beat him. Badly. But there'd been no thrill of victory for Beth. No gloating. Clearly his mind hadn't been on the game.

The next morning, after a sleepless night, Beth went downstairs and set up her easel on the enclosed back porch. The dawn light was still a promise as she dug into the cupboards to find an old canvas.

For a long time she simply stared at the blank piece of stretched fabric in front of her. She plumbed her depths. Were there talents there she hadn't yet explored?

Slowly, and then with more confidence, she began to sketch. The shape of Irene Whitefeather appeared, her distinctive dark eyes, high cheekbones and flashing warm smile, along with the two children who nestled at her side. Deep inside, Beth felt the woman's determination and independence, a mix of her ancestry and the world she faced on a daily basis... and conquered.

A bit of Bengie appeared at the edge of a modest house; the garden was in total disarray. There was hope in the picture. Pathos, too. As Beth's strokes with the charcoal became more confident, she could feel the shredding of one culture into the next.

What would Jason Ambrose think of her sketch? she wondered and then quickly set the thought aside. Even if she was his granddaughter, her style would be her own. She'd simply stretch her own abilities as far as they would go and see what happened.

None of her efforts, however, seemed to change the awful empty feeling deep inside Beth. Hawk would never be hers.

The jangle of the telephone broke her concentration.

Later that morning at the county seat, Hawk leaned his elbow on top of the computer console. "What's happenin', Eddie?" The young woman who clerked for the Sheriff's Department looked less like an "Eddie" than anyone he could think of. To say her proportions were generous was an understatement. Not that anyone would speak the thought aloud. Her husband was the biggest, toughest cowboy Hawk had ever seen this side of Texas.

"Network's as busy as an ant hill on the move," she said, studying the computer screen. "Everybody wants to know somethin' from somebody else."

"You get any information for me yet?"

She glanced up. "On your break-ins?"

"Right. Any of the stolen property turn up?" Hawk knew Eddie played the computer like a concert pianist. If anyone could find a lead in the maze of interlinking police data banks, she was the one.

"Sorry. Zipola as far."

"Too bad." Discouraged, he tipped his hat farther back on his head with his thumb. "Well, keep trying. The thieves are bound to turn the hot goods into cash soon. Somewhere."

Walking down the hallway, nodding distractedly to some of the deputies he knew, Hawk's thoughts shifted to Beth. It wasn't often he gave up on something he wanted. And he *wanted* Beth. Maybe she was the exception that proved the rule.

He'd had to force himself to stay for dinner after he'd finished the window job. And the Scrabble game had been a bust. At best, conversation had been strained. He simply hadn't known what to say. Still didn't.

How the hell do you persuade a woman to do something she was dead set against? He couldn't exactly hold a pistol to her head. And seduction hadn't worked. What the hell was a guy supposed to do?

Rounding a corner, he nearly collided with his boss, Sheriff Ramsey.

"Whoa there, Hawk. Rein in a little."

"Sorry, Sheriff. Guess I wasn't looking where I was going."

"Must be thinkin' about that pretty little filly I heard was back in Newellton."

Hawk scowled. "How'd you hear about that?"

The sheriff laughed. "Son, when you've been in politics as long as I have, you've got all kinds of sources."

The quintessential politician, Rick Ramsey had a quick smile and easy manner that belied a wealth of both experience and intelligence. Since his first election twenty-some years ago, he'd built a solid constituency base while not gaining an inch around his waist from his frequent travels on the chicken-and-peas speaker's circuit. Hawk had to admire all those attributes, as well as the man's skills as a leader. There wasn't a man on the force who wouldn't go out on a limb for the sheriff.

The older man looped his arm around Hawk's shoulders. "Come on into my office, Deputy. I've been meaning to have a talk with you."

Hawk didn't like the sound of that, but he could hardly refuse.

Ramsey's office was about ten times the size of the cubicle Hawk called home. An impressive walnut desk sat near the middle of the room, and a group of chairs surrounded a conference table off to the side. The walls were covered with plaques and photographs featuring Ramsey with political figures from across the country.

"You've been doing a good job out at Newellton," Ramsey said, gesturing for Hawk to take a chair at the conference table.

"Thank you, sir."

"Lay off the 'sir' business for now. This conversation is strictly personal . . . and confidential."

Hawk tensed. Had Beth been right? Was Taylor Franklin behind this friendly little chat the sheriff wanted? The idea rankled more than Hawk would like to admit. His personal life was his own.

Sliding into a chair and casually crossing his ankles, Ramsey said, "Have you ever considered politics?"

It took a moment for the question to sink in. "No, sir . . . Sheriff."

"Call me Rick." He ran his palm across his thinning gray hair. "I haven't announced it yet, but I'm giving some thought to taking up fishing full-time."

"Retiring?" He didn't look, or act, that old.

"The wife and I used to really enjoy cooking up a passel of trout for dinner, settin' ourselves around a fire and just enjoyin' the good ol' outdoors. Haven't had time for that in some years."

"You're a damned good administrator, sir . . . Rick. The department would miss you."

"Not if the right man replaced me. Somebody who had a solid foundation in law enforcement and could gain the respect of all the folks in the county."

Wondering what his boss was up to, Hawk shifted uncomfortably in his chair. "I'm sure there are a lot of senior men in the department—"

"I can think of a couple of the ol' boys who'd love the job... and all the perks that go with it. I'd have trouble backin' any of 'em." He leaned forward and placed his suntanned hands on the table. "What I'm lookin' for is a young guy who's smart enough not to let politics interfere with the job that has to be done. You know anybody like that?"

"Are you suggesting..." Running for political office had never occurred to Hawk. "Me?"

"Don't look so surprised, young man. You've got the credentials. Law degree. Experience on the job. And your Indian ancestry would be a plus. Well-known and respected in the community, too. All you need now is the right backing."

Was he offering Hawk all of his well-oiled political machinery? Those connections and the influence that went with them would practically guarantee election. "I don't know, Rick. I'd have to give it a whole lot of thought."

"I've tried to keep things real open in this county over the years. I want to leave the job to somebody I think could carry on in my footsteps. Makin' his own tracks, too, of course." His pale blue eyes burrowed into Hawk. "I've been keepin' my eye on you since you joined up and I like what I see. It's the kind of job where you could really make a difference, Hawk."

The man sure knew how to dangle a carrot in front of a guy, Hawk thought. Being able to make a difference was a tempting idea. Not that things were so bad in the county now, but there were always underlying racial tensions, and the population was growing fast.

"I'll give it some *serious* thought, Rick. I'm flattered you'd ask."

"Don't be flattered, young man. I'm convinced the future is yours if you're willing to grab it." The sheriff stood and extended his hand. "Get back to me in the next few days. Meanwhile, why don't you hog-tie that little Newellton gal? A married candidate always does much better at the polls than a bachelor."

Hawk held the sheriff's gaze. The guy had to be a mind reader. Sure, he wanted to marry Beth. But how the hell was he going to do that? She was practically on her way back to New York. But run for sheriff? Man, that had come out of the blue.

Considering both ideas, Hawk's lips curled into a half smile. Why not? Never let it be said Hawk didn't try to oblige his employer. At least he'd do his damnedest about the marrying part.

Sheriff Raymond Hawk had a nice ring to it, too.

Chapter Nine

Impatiently Beth yanked the phone receiver from the hook. It was the third call interrupting her painting she'd had that morning. None of them the one she wanted.

"Miss Haggerty?"

The sound of a stranger's voice gnawed at the hollow feeling at the pit of her stomach. She'd hoped it would be Hawk. Not that it would make any difference to their future together. They simply didn't have one. That had been quite clear when he left in a blue funk after the Scrabble game last night.

"Speaking," she responded to the caller.

"My name is George Fitch, Miss Haggerty, of the Bentley Gallery in New York. I understand you have discovered an Ambrose painting."

He and everybody else had discovered the same thing, based on the calls she'd already received. "That's true, Mr. Fitch." She'd never expected the wire service to pick up the story that Millie Russell had so quickly spread to the editor of the local paper. A fellow Garden Club member, no doubt.

"I've booked a flight to Montana this afternoon. I wonder if you would have time to see me about...four o'clock, your time?"

"Really, Mr. Fitch, there's no rush—"

"Miss Haggerty, I have a buyer for the painting and have been authorized to offer you a substantial amount of money, if I am able to authenticate the painting."

"You're welcome to come take a look at it." At least she'd get the opinion of someone in the business. "But I can't guarantee I'll sell. I plan to take my time—"

"I assure you, when you hear my offer you'll be very interested."

"Very well," she said with a sigh. "I'll listen to your offer. But I have a meeting this afternoon and won't be available until about six o'clock."

"I'll be there." The art dealer ended the conversation by getting the directions from the airport to Beth's house.

After hanging up the phone, Beth raked her fingers through her uncombed hair. There was no sense to even try to go back to her sketching. The mood was gone.

Glancing at her watch, she decided she'd work on the attic some more. The number of days left in Newellton was growing short, and she'd have to devote the afternoon to helping Annie Mae and her friends decorate the gym for this evening's dance.

Nostalgia swept over Beth as soon as she stepped into the gym. The place even smelled the same as she remembered, an odd combination of human sweat, mildewing sneakers and floor wax.

A dozen kids laughed and shouted across the echoing expanse of the gym. Several were perched precariously on the top of ladders as they draped old parachutes for a false ceiling between the metal overhead beams. Contributed by a local fire-jumping school, the silk fabric billowed like orange, white and yellow clouds blown by a freshening breeze.

Behind the stand set up for the disc jockey, a banner announced Dancing Through Time, the theme for the party. Below that, a huge cardboard clock with hands all askew provided a backdrop. Two giant video screens loaned by a local business marked either end of the room, camouflaging the basketball hoops.

Beth smiled. The kids were doing a good job. Just as she'd hoped, they'd gotten all the pieces together.

"'Lo, Miss Haggerty," Tommy called to her from a nearby ladder. "What do you think?"

"Looking good. Where are the clocks?"

"Out in my truck. I picked 'em up from the thrift shop but Annie Mae says we gotta get this stuff up first."

"She's right. The clocks are just added accents." Like balloons might be at any other dance.

Finished attaching one side of a parachute, Tommy climbed down the ladder. "You 'n' Sheriff Hawk comin' tonight?"

There certainly were no secrets in Newellton. It hadn't taken long for Beth and Hawk to become "an item," probably with Millie Russell's help.

"Not that I know of," she said. Hawk hadn't mentioned anything about attending the dance. "You guys don't need any more chaperons."

Tommy shifted the ladder to a new position. "Too bad. Hawk's okay. And it wouldn't hurt to have the next county sheriff on our side."

"What do you mean, next? He's already a deputy."

The young man's pimply face suffused with color. "Ah, shoot, I guess I shouldn't have said nuthin'."

Puzzled, Beth braced the ladder to steady his climb. "What are you talking about?"

"Well, see...I got this buddy. His uncle is Sheriff Ramsey. You know, the big cheese over at the county seat. My buddy heard his uncle and his old lady talkin' about Hawk. They're thinkin' about running him for county sheriff." Tommy pulled the corner of the parachute up to a metal beam and attached it with masking tape. "I thought it was a done deal, but maybe they're still just thinking about it."

Beth held Tommy's ladder for a few moments until he climbed down again. Hawk was going to run for county sheriff? Beyond the county commissioners, that was practically the highest elective office around. Certainly the most visible. If he was set on burrowing his roots into the community, being the sheriff was definitely the way to do it.

The gnawing sensation she'd had in her stomach all day started to burn. So did the press of tears at the back of her eyes. She was so darn proud of Hawk! And it hurt so much to know she would never be able to share his successes with him. No one who had political aspirations in this county would want to be connected with a Haggerty girl.

She hung around the gym for a couple more hours, making suggestions about the decorations and how to make the lighting more intimate. Basically Annie Mae and her friends needed little help. With just a bit of encouragement, their own creativity and enthusiasm blossomed.

For a moment as she drove away from the school to make her appointment with the art dealer, she regretted she wouldn't be able to see the completed decorations. Forcefully she set aside the thought. High school dances had never been her thing. Forget how much she would like, just once, to be held in Hawk's arms while they danced.

To her surprise when she arrived home there was not one, but two men waiting for her on the porch.

As she got out of her car, her gaze riveted on Hawk. Dressed in a dark suit, white shirt and muted paisley tie, he simply took her breath away. She'd never seen him look more handsome. He would have fitted into the boardrooms of any city. Only his long hair tied back with a thong marked him as different. Special.

She wished he would let his hair flow freely across his shoulders. Her fingers itched to plow through the thick mane, to feel its weight and texture just once more before she returned to New York.

The guy was absolutely driving her crazy. Or maybe it was her own long-held fantasies. Fantasies that weren't about to come true with a guy who already looked like a successful politician.

With an effort she shifted her gaze to the other man. "Mr. Fitch?"

"Yes. I've come to take a look at the painting," replied the stranger, a frail, elderly man so short he barely came up to Beth's shoulders. He carried a tattered briefcase in his hand.

"Come on in," she invited, pulling open the screen and turning the key in the door. She ignored the sensation of Hawk's nearness and the intoxicating whiff of spicy after-shave she caught when he stopped beside her.

"You're really going to sell the painting?" Hawk asked under his breath.

She shrugged. "The guy wanted to see it." Her heart doing an irregular beat against her ribs, she hurried past him into the house.

After retrieving the portrait from the hall closet, Beth propped it on the living-room couch.

"Ah," the art dealer commented, sounding like someone who had just tasted a rich dessert for the first time. With a magnifying glass to his eye, Fitch bent closer to study the painting.

All during the examination, Beth was aware of Hawk moving restlessly around the room. He was like a caged lion, and she felt his eyes on her every moment. Her flesh heated under his intense scrutiny; her heart thudded a heavy beat. Occasionally Hawk's gaze switched to Fitch and he scowled.

What was Hawk thinking about? she wondered. And why was he so dressed up? Lord, he looked so good she wanted to grab him and hold on tight before some other woman realized what a good catch he'd be. Of course, she couldn't do that.

"Beth, could I talk to you?" With a jerky lift of his chin, Hawk indicated she should follow him to the far side of the room out of the art dealer's earshot.

"What's wrong?" she asked in a hushed voice.

"Do you know this art dealer?"

"I've heard of the Bentley Gallery. I think I've even visited there once."

"He's kind of a smarmy character." Something about him made Hawk's skin crawl. All the time they'd waited together on Beth's front porch, his law enforcement instincts had been sounding a red alert.

"It looks to me like he knows his business."

Hawk wasn't convinced. "Did you ask for identification?"

"He gave me his card."

"Anyone can have a phony business card printed up," Hawk pointed out. "And there are a lot of con men operating in the art business."

"I don't intend to take the first offer I get, if that's what is bothering you."

"Sometimes you tend to be a bit impulsive," he reminded her, narrowing his eyes.

He unbuttoned his jacket and let it hang open. The art dealer wasn't the only thing bothering him. He had his own plans for this evening, and he didn't want any distractions. Slipping his hand in his pants pocket, he gripped the small velvet box he'd picked up at a jewelry store that afternoon. His plans definitely didn't involve rousting some fraudulent art dealer.

"If you decide to sell," Hawk said, "I want you to insist on a certified check from a major bank. Then I want you to confirm with the bank that it's good."

"My, we are being suspicious, aren't we?" The sparkle in her eyes teased him.

"It's my job, Beth." He had an urge to protect her from more than just crooks. He wanted to stand between her and guys like Taylor Franklin or anyone else who spoke unkindly of her. No bunch of hoodlums would dare corner her in a bank parking lot or vandalize her home if Beth belonged to him. He could give her status and acceptance in the community, all the things he'd worked so hard to obtain. The county sheriff could do that.

If she would have him.

She looked so damn sexy in her tank top with an overblouse that managed to conceal very little of her attributes. His need for her twisted through his loins.

He tried not to think about that. Not just yet. Later that evening would do him just fine.

Fitch finished examining the painting. "No question, Miss Haggerty. An Ambrose in excellent condition. You are a very fortunate young woman." His narrow lips separated into a smile, revealing yellowed teeth.

"I was pretty sure it was authentic," Beth agreed, pleased he'd confirmed the artist. She smiled fondly at the portrait. Dear Grandma Claire. What a time she must have had. It seemed almost sacrilegious to sell the one item that must have represented both heartache and love to her grandmother.

"Now, Miss Haggerty, as to the amount my buyer wishes to offer...."

The figure Fitch named sent a rush of blood to Beth's head. In her wildest dreams, she'd never imagined she'd have that much money in her entire life. Certainly not all in one lump sum.

"She'd expect a certified check," Hawk insisted grimly.

"I assure you, Mr. Hawk, that won't be necessary." Fitch lifted his briefcase onto the couch, unlocked it, and opened the lid.

Astounded, Beth stared at the array of neatly bundled bills filling nearly the entire briefcase. "Cash?" The word came out as little more than a croak.

"That's a lot of money to be carrying around," Hawk said. He picked up one of the packs and flipped through the bills. If he'd been concerned before that something wasn't quite right, now he smelled a full-fledged rat.

"We find cash transactions are very fast and efficient," Fitch said.

"I just bet you do." Hawk tossed the pack of twenties back into the briefcase and closed the lid. "Miss Haggerty will keep your offer in mind."

"I will?" Beth choked on the word and coughed.

"Obviously, Mr. Hawk, I would like to close the deal now and be on my way back to New York with the painting for my client."

And to pick up some nice laundered drug money when they resold the portrait, Hawk suspected.

He took Fitch firmly by the arm.

"Now see here, young man. I won't be bullied. Miss Haggerty should understand—"

"Miss Haggerty will call you if she decides to accept your offer," he said, escorting the man and his briefcase to the door.

"Hawk, what are you doing?" Beth hissed. "That's more money than—"

"Than it's worth." He closed the door behind the sputtering art dealer.

Beth planted her fists on her hips. "Raymond Hawk! You had no right to send that man away."

He grinned at the stubborn lift of her chin. "You weren't going to take the first offer, anyway. Remember?"

"But he said—"

"Slow down, Beth. Think a minute. What kind of people do business with that much cash?"

She frowned. "Was it counterfeit?"

"Nope. All used bills."

He watched her face as she considered the alternatives. Slowly, realization dawned and her eyes widened with alarm. "Drug money?"

"That would be my guess."

"I just can't believe... Bentley Gallery has been around for ages. Maybe you were right. He was probably just using their name." She set her jaw at a grim, determined angle. "No way would I sell my grandmother to a *drug* dealer."

Hawk laughed from low in his gut. "Just who would you like to sell her to?"

"Why, I want to find her a good home, of course."

"I see." He rubbed his palm along his jaw. "A nice family with three kids, two dogs and a cat who would appreciate her."

"Well, something like that, I suppose. After all, Ambrose or not, this *is* my grandmother. At least, it's a painting of her. I certainly wouldn't want to see her hanging behind the bar of some sleazy tavern, much less on the wall of some guy's office who sells dope."

"Then why don't you keep her, Beth?" he asked softly. Together they could come up with the kids and pets to round out the family portrait.

Her gaze shifted away from his as though she'd read his mind and rejected the idea. "I'd like to, Hawk. I just don't think I can." The regret in her voice twisted as painfully as a spear impaled in his heart.

Hawk walked across the room and re-draped the portrait with its dust cover. If Grandma Claire were still around, maybe the ol' gal could have given him some good advice. Without her, it looked like Hawk was on his own. "I think it would be best if we kept this locked up at my office."

"You think somebody might steal it?"

Turning, he smiled. "Better safe than sorry. Meanwhile, you'd better get yourself all fancied up." He checked his watch. "We've got dinner reservations in forty-five minutes and it's a long drive."

"Dinner?" she echoed.

"At that nice place on Central in the county seat. And then we're going to the dance."

"At the school?"

"It's the least I can do. You missed a lot of high school dances when you were young, and I intend to make up for that tonight."

"You don't have to—"

Purposefully he sauntered to where she stood and looked down into her puzzled green eyes. "After that, we may consider Lover's Gulch...."

"That's for kids." Color rose on her cheeks and she licked her lips.

"For more adult entertainment we could consider your bedroom upstairs."

"Hawk, I don't think—"

He cut off her words with his mouth. Her lips were soft, hot, moist against his. Sweet heaven, she tasted good. His tongue slipped between the seam of her lips. Velvet heat. He heard a small moan of pleasure escape from her throat and his groin muscles tightened. God, he wanted this woman!

She pressed her hands against his chest and he backed off, his heart beating like a tom-tom. He fisted the rich strands of her thick, silky hair, fighting the groan of frustration that threatened. "On the other hand," he suggested hoarsely, "we could forget all about dinner."

"Nooo..." Beth sobbed, slipping away from his grasp. It was all she could do not to succumb to the temptation of Hawk. At this point the better part of valor was to accept his invitation to dinner. Then she'd deal with the subsequent events—when her knees didn't feel quite so weak and the arrowed heat his hungry kiss had sent through her body had cooled considerably.

As if those feelings would ever dim, she thought, as she hurried upstairs to change.

In contrast to the other women in the restaurant, Beth had looked like a vibrant bird of paradise. She'd piled her hair on top of her head, her curls barely restrained by a narrow, colorful scarf. Her low-cut blouse and full, softly pleated skirt were just as brilliant, in shades that had turned every head in the room, particularly the men.

Hawk hadn't liked that. He'd had in mind a quiet, intimate dinner for two. Not a whole roomful of leering guys, who were as busy mentally undressing Beth as he was.

Now he was faced with a writhing mob of teenagers and music so loud he couldn't hear himself think.

"Isn't this great!" Beth cried, dragging him by the hand into the gym.

"It's too loud," he shouted.

"What? I can't hear you."

"Nothing," he grumbled. He definitely hadn't thought his plan through clearly enough. This was a hell of a place to expect any kind of intimacy. All he'd wanted to do was hold her in his arms for a little slow dancing, warm her up a bit and then take her back home where he could propose and thoroughly seduce her. The order of the latter two activities didn't matter to him.

Her cheeks flushed with excitement, Beth stood on tiptoe and shouted into his ear. "How do you like the decorations?"

"Kind of surrealistic, don't you think?" Clocks of every shape and size dangled from the false ceiling along with metallic streamers that caught the flare of strobe lights flashing at irregular intervals. Larger than life characters danced across the two video screens at either end of the gym. To Hawk, the whole thing looked carefully designed to create an instant headache.

"The kids wanted some action, so that's what they got." She tugged on his hand. "Come on. Let's dance."

Hawk decided the gyrations these kids were doing could only marginally be called dancing. He was more a two-step kind of guy.

"Let's wait for a slow one," he suggested over the blare of the loud speakers.

"Don't be such a stick-in-the-mud." Grinning up at him, Beth started her hips and shoulders undulating in time to the music.

"I don't know how to dance like that." Neither should she. It was too damn suggestive by far. Her motions set off an instant and heated reaction in his body.

"That's what the videos are for. If you don't know the steps, you just check the screen." She thrust her hips toward him for several beats, effectively mimicking an act that should be done only in private.

Hawk felt perspiration bead on his forehead. "Knock it off, Beth. Is that what you learned in New York?"

"Among other things." Her smile faded. "I thought we came here to dance, Hawk."

"You dance like these kids are doing, and you'll have the whole town talking for sure."

She looked at him for a long time, her expression a mask. "I am who I am, Hawk. I came here to have a good time and that's exactly what I intend to do. If that doesn't please you..." She lifted her shoulders in a gesture of resignation.

He hesitated. Damn, he did want to dance with her. But not like this. And not in front of all these kids.

Before he had a chance to respond, she whirled away, her full skirt riding up to show her well-shaped thighs, and she walked purposefully into the middle of the dance floor. A minute later she'd been intercepted by the star linebacker of the football team and they were gyrating with their bodies pressed tightly together.

Hawk backed off to the side of the room, silently cursing himself as he went. He found the punch bowl and downed two cups in quick succession, never once taking his eyes off Beth.

He wanted very much to feel Beth's body thrusting against him, to have his arms around her and feel her heat and soft body along the length of his. He wanted to feel her weight as she leaned back, lifting her breasts and baring her throat for his kisses. He wanted her vulnerable and sexy in his arms.

Now some other guy held her. Granted, he was just a punk kid of no more than eighteen. But that didn't matter. Anger and jealousy still knotted in Hawk's stomach.

Grudgingly he admitted Beth wasn't doing anything different than any other girl in the crowd was doing. Even so, she stood out from the rest like a glittering star on a dark night. Her cheeks were flushed, her eyes alight with pleasure. Tendrils of hair had escaped from the restraint of her scarf to lie in soft, damp curls at her nape and ears.

He felt a primal urge uncoil hotly within him. He wanted to toss Beth Haggerty over his shoulder, carry her out of this madhouse and make love to her so long and so fast she'd never look at another guy again.

It was when the football jock let his hands slip up from Beth's waist dangerously close to her breasts that Hawk decided he'd had enough. He fisted the empty paper cup into a ball and tossed it hard into the trash.

Oblivious to everyone else on the dance floor, Hawk shoved his way through the crowd.

Beth saw him coming. From the angry look in his dark eyes, she suspected he was mad enough to take somebody's scalp. Probably hers.

Her retreating partner left her alone to face Hawk. She lifted her chin. "I trust you've decided to dance."

"It's time to go home, Beth. You're making a spectacle of yourself."

"Sorry. You go ahead. I'll catch a ride with one of the kids." Or walk if she had to. She wasn't going to let Hawk spoil her evening. Nor was he going to order her around.

She turned away but he grabbed her by the arm and spun her back to him. "All right, damn it! I'll dance."

"Good."

"You'll have to show me the steps."

He could bet his blasted badge that's just what she was going to do. If Hawk had thought she'd been making a scene so far, just let him watch her smoke now. On second thought, the little imp on her shoulder suggested, maybe she could make *him* smoke and smolder a bit.

"Okay," she agreed, lifting her arms to his shoulders. "Put your hands on my hips. Now, do what I do." She rotated side to side, then thrust her hips forward.

"Geez, Beth..."

"Loosen up, Hawk. Relax your knees. You won't break." But maybe she could get him to bend a little. "Don't think about your body. Let it flow with the music. Watch my eyes."

Hawk tried. How in God's name was he supposed to concentrate on her eyes when all he could think about was his *body* and hers? Her leg pressed insistently between his thighs, and he rode her with every beat. His hands had found the softness of her buttocks. In spite of his best intentions, he grabbed a handful of soft fabric and flesh, and felt her muscles tighten as she rolled her hips against him. His awareness settled at that point of contact with fiery intensity.

"Beth, we can't—"

"You're doing fine."

Her smug grin suggested she knew exactly the effect she was having on him. It would be hard for her not to know. *Hard* being the operative word, Hawk thought grimly.

She did a switch on him, turning so she spooned her rotating hips against his groin. He caught a whiff of her seductive perfume and heat rocketed through his entire body. Sweat edged down his temples. The music pulsated in his gut.

God, she was driving him wild.

He was vaguely aware of hoots and hollers somewhere nearby, and that there were no other dancers around. It took all of his efforts to keep up with Beth's gyrations and keep himself under some semblance of control.

A moment later she was behind him, doing the same thing to his butt she'd done to his front, her hands stroking along his shoulders and neck until he felt his hair loosened from its thong. What the hell—

He whirled and pulled her hard against his chest. She was a devil! Caught up in the swirl of sensations, he bent her back and crossed her mouth with a deep, hungry kiss that she returned with a sensual fury that very nearly cost him the few remaining shreds of his self-control.

The sudden silence that followed reverberated in Hawk's head. The damn DJ had chosen that moment to end the music and take a break.

Panting, he looked around at two hundred grinning teenagers. Every one of them started to applaud.

"Come on," he growled, pulling Beth upright and taking her by the wrist. By morning every person in the county would know what they'd been up to. "We're getting out of here."

Beth tried to dig in her heels, but it didn't do any good. He was way too powerful to resist. The only thing that stopped their escape was Annie Mae standing in their path.

"Hey, you guys were great," she said. "I didn't know you could dance like that, Beth."

"I don't usually," she admitted under her breath, which was coming hard and fast. In an odd way she'd been as carried away as Hawk. In her heart she'd been making love to him on the dance floor in front of everyone, she admitted, because she knew she didn't dare do it for real. Hot and urgent love that she would never have a chance to experience. This night had sealed her fate as nothing else before it had.

"You're not leaving, are you?" Annie Mae asked. "I mean there's still time—"

"We're going home," Hawk announced in a tone that didn't invite argument.

Beth had no chance to argue as Hawk dragged her unceremoniously out of the gym.

"Now wait just one darn minute," Beth said, refusing to go an inch further with the big bully.

"I've waited long enough."

"And you're going to wait a whole hell of a lot longer." She knew just what he had in mind if he took her home. Thoughts that weren't all that different from her own. But she had enough sense to know how much she'd suffer in the aftermath. "Will you please stop a minute and think?"

"About what, for God's sake?"

"That we simply aren't right for each other."

He halted like she'd hit him in the stomach with a baseball bat. "How can you say that?"

"You're stodgy, Hawk. So conservative you're absolutely brittle."

"That's not true."

"You didn't want me dancing like that because you think people will talk. About me. About you. All because of a perfectly innocent way to have fun. And your precious reputation would be ruined."

"There's nothing wrong with wanting to be accepted in a community."

"You're right, of course."

"We'd be good together," he said more softly.

"I'm not talking about sex, Hawk. I'm talking about us, together, and how I'd fit into your life."

"You'd fit into my bed just fine. That's all that matters."

"Is it, Hawk? Really?" Her heart suddenly felt very heavy in her chest. "At the restaurant I knew you wished I looked more like those other women who were so subdued and restrained. Neat little dresses. Bland smiles on their faces."

"That's not so."

"Yes, it is. I could see it in your eyes. Don't deny it."

"You could dress differently and nobody would notice you."

"No, of course they wouldn't. And I'd hate myself for being a fraud. I like colors, Hawk. Bright and cheerful and full of life. It took me a lot of years to discover who and what I am, and I won't give up my sense of myself."

"It doesn't matter. Damn it, I love you."

Beth's heart felt like it was breaking into a thousand shards of glass. He might think he loved her, but he couldn't accept her for what she was—her style, her colors, even her occasional impulsive flings. "Would you still feel that way if you were the county sheriff?" A position so visible he'd always be in the limelight.

He frowned. "Where did you hear about that?"

"Haven't you figured out yet just how fast news travels around here?" She palmed Hawk's cheek, simply because she couldn't resist touching him. "I wouldn't be any good for you...or the image you're so proud of. You've worked hard, Hawk. I'm enormously proud of you." She bit her lip to stop her chin from quivering. She wished so much for him and hoped he, at least, would never change. "You'll make a wonderful sheriff."

"Beth, I don't want to lose you again. I'm talking marriage."

Oh, God, marriage. To Hawk. A dream come true. But a nightmare in the making, if he couldn't accept her as she was.

She closed her eyes for a moment, searching her depths to find the strength to make the right decision. For Hawk.

"I'm sorry." The words came out in a whisper because she couldn't find her voice.

His mouth narrowed into a grim line. "So am I." Pain laced his tone.

"Refusals hurt. I know that. But it's the right thing, Hawk. You'll find someone else." Every sane woman in town would jump at the chance to marry Hawk. Except Beth. "You'll survive." She wasn't so sure she would.

Chapter Ten

Beth lengthened her jogging stride along the gravel shoulder of the country road. Morning sun flashed through the few trees that dotted the grassland. She wasn't going to think about the past. Or the future. Or Hawk. She'd run until she couldn't run any farther. Then she'd go back to the house and finish packing.

She still had the real estate agent to see about listing the house for sale. And the man from the antique store was due.

She would keep so busy, get herself so tired, she'd be too numb to be able to think. Until she got back to New York. Then it would be too late.

The road followed a bend in the river, and she startled a couple of magpies from their perch on a low-growing bush. Above the narrow bands of water that slid through a jumble of sandbars, a hawk hovered in the updraft created by a sharp rise in the landscape.

Hawks—powerful, confident. Just like the man who carried the same name.

Her breathing labored, she struggled up the incline.

Around the next turn she noticed Tommy Russell's pickup parked in a clearing off to the side of the road. She'd never seen the kids parked in this particular spot before, but young love was something else she wasn't going to think about. Not now. Not when the hurt she felt was so painfully raw.

She ran by the truck without looking inside, following the road past a couple of abandoned gold mines and a crumbling sod house, until she came to a country highway that would take her back home.

Two days since the dance. Obviously Hawk had accepted the fact that they weren't right for each other. She hadn't heard a word from him. Didn't expect to. But dear God, it hurt!

It was midafternoon when she heard a knock at the door. Thinking it was probably the overdue antique dealer, Beth struggled to her feet, made her way around heaps of packing boxes and hurried down from the attic.

She opened the door to find Millie Russell standing on her porch.

"Oh, hello, dear. I'm so sorry to bother you. I know how busy you must be."

"No problem." Although Beth wasn't eager for a long conversation with Millie, the woman did look troubled, pacing back and forth across the porch and peering down the street as if expecting the devil himself to appear. "Is there something I can do for you?"

"Oh, no. Nothing like that." Millie shoved some wisps of snowy white hair out of her eyes. "I just wondered if today was the day Tommy is supposed to mow your grass."

"No. He's scheduled for tomorrow."

Millie's hands fluttered around her face like butterflies with no place to go. "I'm sure there's nothing wrong."

Beth didn't like the sound of that. "Has something happened to Tommy?"

"I don't think so. I mean, he's a good boy. It's just that...well, he wasn't in school today and nobody's seen him. His father's very upset."

Beth imagined cutting classes did that to a parent. "I'm sure he'll turn up." Surely those two kids weren't still necking out by the river road. She'd seen them hours ago. And she didn't want to tell Millie. Beth made it a point never to spread gossip about anyone, particularly young people. In this case learning that Tommy spent more time with Annie Mae than he probably should would certainly fuel parental ire.

"Well, if you see him—"

"I'll let you know."

Since Millie appeared a little unsteady on her feet, Beth took her elbow to help her down the porch steps. As she did she noticed the curtains shift in the house across the street and a shadow appear in the window.

Beth frowned. "Millie, is there anyone at your house now?"

"Oh, no, dear. It's just Charlie and me at home. You're welcome to come visit, if you'd like. Just the other day I bought some nice mint tea. That was my Arnold's favorite. If you'd like a cup—"

"No, I... Then who is that at your window?"

Millie glanced across the street. "That's just my Charlie. He's such a nosy old bird. Never lets a thing go on in this neighborhood without him seeing it. I have to leave his perch right by the window or he raises such a fuss a body simply can't stand it."

"I see." And suddenly Beth did see. More clearly than she had in years. How many other incorrect assumptions had she drawn? she wondered. "But sometimes you look out the window, too."

"Land's sake," she laughed. "I don't have much time for frittering away the day looking out the window. There's the thrift shop and the Garden Club to keep me busy. I'm on the board of practically every nonprofit around. And the Grange fall social is coming. We're raising money for a new baseball diamond. Do wish you were going to be around for that. It's quite a party."

"I'm sure it is." One that was likely to need posters made to help with the advertising, Beth thought with a smile.

Blowing out a sigh, she watched Millie cross the street. Could she have misjudged the woman? It hardly seemed possible. Millie seemed to know so much about what was going on in town, Beth would have guessed her nose was always pressed to the window glass. But maybe she'd been wrong.

That possibility still troubled Beth as she went back to work in the attic. So did the fact that Tommy, and probably Annie Mae, were among the missing.

As she sorted out the last of Grandma's personal effects from a big oak dresser, Beth's thoughts shifted back to the high school dance and just how cute Annie Mae had looked. An adorable girl right on the verge of becoming a woman. She'd been wearing

tastefully applied makeup that accented her good features, well-defined cheekbones and full lips. The girl
had chosen a soft, persimmon shade of lip gloss that
went beautifully with her complexion. Little wonder
Tommy was attracted to Annie Mae.

Beth pulled her lower lip between her teeth, her
hands stilling as she held a nearly empty dresser drawer
over a trash bin. There was something about—

The drawer slipped from her grasp.

Dear God, not Annie Mae and Tommy, she prayed.
They were such nice kids. Surely her judgment of
people wasn't that far out of kilter.

A tightness banded her chest.

As much as she hated to, she'd have to call Hawk.
He'd know what to do.

Her fingers trembled as she dialed the phone.

"Sheriff's office. Hawk speaking."

She fought the constriction in her throat. She was
going to miss him so much. "Hawk, it's me."

For a long moment the silence was deafening on the
other end of the line. "Hello, Beth," he responded
tautly.

He had every right to be upset, even angry with her,
but Beth simply didn't have time to deal with that right
now. "Millie Russell came over a little while ago. She
said no one has seen Tommy all day. His parents are
worried."

"Do they think he's run away?" Surprise laced his
words. "The kid has to be seventeen, eighteen years
old. He's probably cut out to go hunting. The season
just started— "

"No, I don't think so." The area where she'd seen
the pickup had been posted with No Trespassing signs,
and it wasn't especially good deer country, anyway. "I

saw his truck this morning, Hawk. Out along the river road. When I was jogging. I just assumed ... I mean, I thought he and Annie Mae were—"

"Yeah, I know. Their hormones have been working overtime."

Beth remembered when she and Hawk had experienced the same sensation. Ten years ago ... and then more recently. "I'm worried, Hawk. It's been all day."

"I'll take a drive out that way and have a look around."

Her hand folded more tightly around the phone. "There's something else you need to know."

He hesitated a moment. "What's that?"

"The lipstick Annie Mae was wearing two nights ago. It was the same persimmon shade used by the vandals who broke into Grandma Claire's house. It's what they used to write the message on the mirror."

The pause was longer this time, and Beth could almost hear Hawk thinking.

"There've got to be thousands of women who wear any particular shade of lipstick," he said. "It probably doesn't mean anything."

"It's a very unusual color. Very distinctive, and trust me, once I see a color, I never forget it. That particular shade doesn't work for every woman, but it certainly did for Annie Mae."

She heard him swear under his breath. "There are a whole hell of a lot of old mine shafts and natural caves along the river bank. Plenty of places to hide stolen goods."

"Oh, Hawk, I just can't believe—"

"I'll check it out and let you know."

"I'll meet you there—"

"No. This isn't your concern."

"The heck it isn't. I blew the whistle on those kids."
In some ways, against her better judgment. "It will
take me less than ten minutes to get to the river road."

Somehow Hawk got there first. He was already
standing beside Tommy's truck when Beth slid her
grandmother's old Rambler to a stop. Her heart
squeezed tight at the sight of him.

Straightening her shoulders and lifting her chin, she
got out of the car. Her pride demanded that she not let
him know just how much she hated the thought of
never seeing him again.

When he turned, his eyes were dark, his expression
unreadable in the shade cast by the brim of his hat.

"No sign of them," he said, his voice firm and
controlled, as though she were an ordinary stranger
who just happened to report a missing person. "When
you saw the truck this morning, did you actually see
Tommy, too?"

"No," she admitted. "I didn't really look." She'd
been hurting too badly to want to see a couple in love.

They stood there a minute in silence, only the chill-
ing wind carrying on a conversation with the dry,
winter grass. Beth shivered and pulled her short jacket
more tightly around her.

Dropping his gaze, Hawk eyed the ground around
the truck. He couldn't think about Beth right now, not
how she looked so vulnerable standing there with the
wide expanse of prairie behind her or how much he
wanted to take her in his arms. She'd made the decision about their future—a decision he'd simply have
to learn to live with. His only concern right now was
Tommy Russell and probably Annie Mae.

He walked slowly around the truck looking for signs. There'd been no struggle as near as he could tell. But here and there rocks and gravel had shifted since the last rain. Footprints. But whose?

There'd been another vehicle parked here recently. Maybe another truck from the looks of the tire tracks. But then, this was the kind of secluded spot where almost anybody might stop to take care of something as simple as the call of nature. It wasn't a highly traveled road. In fact, as he thought about it, he ought to warn Beth not to jog alone in this remote area. She'd be better off closer to town. Not that it mattered, he realized, fighting off a new wave of regret. She'd be gone soon enough.

As he walked to the opposite side of the road above the river, he was aware of Beth following him, her footsteps making soft, crunching sounds on the gravel. She was light on her feet, light in his arms. And he couldn't think about that.

He scanned the opposite bank, not quite sure what he hoped to spot. Geologically it was an odd combination of sandstone and granite that had been unsuccessfully mined for ore around the turn of the century. Along the river's edge, it was definitely unstable ground.

A slight movement of dirt and rocks caught his eye. Then he realized what he'd been looking for.

A fresh landslide.

Slipping and sliding, his adrenaline pumping hard, he headed down the near bank to the river.

"What are you doing, Hawk?" Beth called.

"I've got to check something out." He splashed into the shallow water. On the first sandbar he spotted footprints. A couple of sets of tennis shoes and some work boots. Not fishermen this time of year. The water was too low except in the deepest pools well upstream.

He heard Beth right behind him.

"You stay up by the car," he ordered.

"Not on your life. I'm right behind you."

He quirked his lips. Stubborn woman. Somebody ought to teach her a little respect, too. Slanting her a glance, Hawk found he was doubly sorry he couldn't be the one.

Once at the landslide he moved gingerly around the edges, not wanting to loosen any more dirt. From the looks of the few bushes that had come down with the rocks, the slide had happened in the last twenty-four hours. The upturned roots were still damp. If those kids were in a cave behind that wall of scree, it wouldn't be easy to get them out.

He picked up a fist-size rock. Moving cautiously, he made his way to the middle of the slide. His efforts caused more debris to slip down the hill, rocks clinking together and dust trails puffing up.

"Be careful," Beth called.

With the rock, he tapped a larger boulder several times. The sound echoed loudly in the stillness along the river. When he heard no response, he tried again. Come on, Tommy. Be there.

Then he heard it. A faint response from somewhere behind the mound of dirt.

Hot damn! Somebody was inside. Alive.

Hitting the boulder again, Hawk let them know he'd heard them by repeating the rhythm of their tapping. "Hang in there, kids," he shouted, though he wasn't sure they could hear his voice. "Help is on the way."

Forcing himself not to hurry, he climbed down the scree. "Beth, I want you to get on my car radio."

"You've found them?"

"I think so. Tell dispatch we're going to need men, shovels and some lumber for bracing."

Beth placed her hand lightly on his arm. "Are they okay?"

Resisting the urge to fold his fingers over hers, Hawk said, "We won't know till we get them out." He couldn't even be sure it was the kids, one or both of them. And uninjured. For all he knew, it could be someone else entirely, though that didn't seem reasonable. But he'd been surprised before.

"I should have called you earlier." Withdrawing her hand, Beth was swept with feelings of guilt. Guilt for not being the right woman for Hawk, guilt for not telling Millie where her grandson was. Maybe Beth couldn't change who she was—which meant she'd never be conservative enough to be the sheriff's wife—but she could have helped a neighbor.

Not wanting Hawk to see the tears that suddenly pooled in her eyes, she turned away and raced back across the river and up the bank to the Jeep. By the time she got back, Hawk was already working methodically on top of the landslide tossing rocks aside.

"Help's coming. They're sending an ambulance, too," she reported, her breath coming hard. She stooped to pick up a rock.

"You'd better stay clear," Hawk warned. An arrow of sweat had already darkened the back of his khaki shirt. "We could get another slide."

"It's no more dangerous for me than it is for you." She'd rather be buried under a ton of rocks with Hawk than to watch him be killed in front of her own eyes.

If her dreams had come true, they would have found some way to grow old together and live out the rest of their lives in each other's arms. But that dream wasn't going to happen. She'd simply take her chances with Hawk now and try not to think about tomorrow or the airplane ticket that was tucked in the pocket of her suitcase.

Hawk muttered something under his breath she couldn't decipher but she kept on working. Suddenly her feet shifted beneath her. She grabbed for something to hang on to and slipped halfway down the slope.

"Damn it, Beth, I told you—"

"I'm all right." She scrambled back into position. "Just worry about the kids."

"Be careful," he ordered gruffly. She knew his angry tone was only because he cared about the youngsters and feared for her safety, too.

"Hawk, I'm sorry about some of the things I said the other night." She grunted with the effort to roll an extra large boulder out of the way. "I hope . . . I hope we can still be friends." Lovers would have been better, but a distant friendship was all she could expect.

"Yeah. Sure. You were probably right about me. Stodgy."

She winced at her own word being thrown back in her face. She hadn't meant to hurt him. Wished that he could loosen up a bit, but knew he'd struggled hard to make his place in the community. She wouldn't take that away from him.

Jagged rocks cut into her palms. Perspiration edged down her temple. Her arms grew weary. Still, one by one she tossed rocks off to the side and Hawk did the same.

"Hawk, is there any chance the kids could suffocate in there?"

He hesitated a long time before answering. "I don't think so. Not if we get to them soon."

Beth shoved at another rock. If only she had acted sooner....

"Maybe we should have asked for a bulldozer," she suggested.

He grunted. "Too dangerous. We'd likely as not cause another slide."

Drawing on all of her strength, she renewed her efforts.

To her relief, a few minutes later there were a dozen other pairs of hands to help. She recognized the owner of Hank's Hardware, the barber and even the guy who ran the tavern just outside of town. Word of the crisis must have spread like a prairie fire. And everyone had come to help, shovels in hand and their pickups filled with lumber.

Giving way to both fatigue and stronger backs, Beth retreated. Hawk had the men organized like a well-disciplined army. No one objected to his authority. He was a natural, well-respected leader. Beth knew every single volunteer would happily vote for Hawk for county sheriff. So would she, though she'd never get the chance.

At the edge of the river, Myrtle Symington greeted her. "Here you go, dear. Something cold to drink."

Hesitantly Beth accepted the plastic container of juice. From the looks of the cardboard cartons stacked around Myrtle's feet, it looked as if she had become a one-woman Red Cross relief station.

"Thank you."

NOT THE MARRYING KIND 161

"The town ladies will be along soon with sand-wiches," Myrtle said. "Just in case, well . . . if it takes a while to get the job done, the boys up there will get hungry. We don't want 'em to run out of steam till those kids are safe."

Beth glanced at the landslide, hoping against hope the kids were all right. "How did everyone hear so fast?" And why were they so willing to leave their jobs and businesses?

"It doesn't take long for word to spread. That's one of the nice things about a small town. If someone needs help, we kin come runnin' lickety-split."

"But what about your grocery store? Surely you didn't just close up."

Myrtle waved off the question as though her store were of no consequence. "I just posted a note saying for folks to leave the money on the counter, or to tell me what they owed, and I'd take care of it when I got back."

"What about strangers? Would you trust them to—"

"There aren't any strangers in Newellton, honey." Myrtle's beady eyes squinted nearly closed when she laughed aloud. "Leastwise, not after the first five minutes or so."

More thirsty than she had realized, Beth took a long swallow of the cherry-flavored drink. What Myrtle said was true. Everyone in Newellton knew the other guy's business. In this case it had certainly paid off. If they'd had to rely on help arriving from the county seat it might have taken hours. Instead of that, the lo-cal folks helped their own.

Myrtle looked Beth up and down. "Guess you de-cided not to open a strip joint in town."

Beth choked on the juice. "No. It didn't work out."

A spark appeared in Myrtle's pale eyes that was somewhere between mischief and envy. "Too bad. Sure would've given us somethin' to talk about. And I heard tell you're a real good dancer."

"Are you talking about the school dance?" And the scene she'd made over Hawk's strenuous objections.

"Yep. The kids really had a good time. Guess they think you're pretty cool, or whatever the expression is this year."

Before Beth could decide if Myrtle's words were praise or criticism, she heard a loud chorus of cheers from the workmen.

"We got 'em," one man shouted. "Tommy and Annie Mae. They're okay."

From all up and down the river, onlookers hurrahed and waved their hats.

Beth smiled and fought back a new upwelling of tears. The entire town had turned out. And they weren't just curious, she realized. They'd been ready to do anything to help.

Impulsively Beth turned around and gave Myrtle a big hug.

"Children!" Myrtle grumbled gruffly, clinging to Beth in a fierce hug of her own, then wiping a tear from her eye. "They give you nothin' but grief."

"They'll be glad to see you. I'm sure they'll be thirsty. Hungry, too."

"Humph. Always thinkin' about themselves. Just like you were at that age. 'Course, I did bring a few cans of root beer along. That's Tommy's favorite." The corners of the old woman's lips lifted into a wry imitation of a smile. "You always liked that cherry stuff when you were feeling low."

Astonished Myrtle had even noticed, much less remembered, Beth looked at the woman with new eyes. Why, the ol' busybody was a softy inside. She'd never realized ...

A few moments later, two tired, dirty teenagers were helped down the hill. Annie Mae leaned heavily on the man who had his arm around her waist, and Tommy had a streak of dried blood on his cheek. Other than that, they both seemed okay, to Beth's great relief.

Both youngsters gratefully accepted the cold drinks Myrtle pressed into their hands and sank onto the ground.

Hawk slipped up beside Beth.

"It's a natural cave that collapsed," he said quietly. "It looks like all the stolen goods from the break-ins are inside. There are several TVs and VCRs. I'm sure your grandmother's things are there."

As Beth looked at the two young people, she felt a heaviness in her heart. Annie's sweet, young face was streaked with dirty tears. Tommy's expression was grim.

"Why, Tommy?" she asked. "And Annie Mae? If you'd needed the money...someone would have helped. You didn't have to steal." With new understanding, Beth realized the townspeople would truly have done what they could for one of their own.

Annie Mae's dark eyes darted from Beth to Hawk and then down to the ground. "Tommy didn't have anything to do with this. It's all—" her chin puckered "—my fault."

Stunned by the girl's confession, Beth knelt next to her. "Are you saying you're the one who's been breaking in to all the houses in town? Including mine?"

Tommy's arm moved protectively around Annie Mae's shoulders. "You gotta tell 'em, hon."

Annie Mae lifted her head. New tears made tracks through the dirt on her cheeks. "I wouldn't steal. Not from anyone. Honest, I wouldn't." Her breath hitched. "It was my Pa." Sobbing, she buried her face in her hands.

In an instinctive gesture of both caring and relief, Beth wrapped her arms around the young woman. "Shh, honey. It's not your fault."

"But it is," Annie Mae wailed. "I was always telling Pa about my friends' houses and how nice they were. They had such nice things and I wanted— If he could've just gotten a decent job..." She hiccuped. "I even told him Grandma Millie said there were treasures in your house. I didn't expect..."

"It's all right, honey. You didn't do anything wrong." Beth swallowed the lump in her throat. Poor kid. All she'd wanted was a decent life. Something her alcoholic father hadn't been able to give her. "Annie Mae, I hate to put you on the spot, but did your father know I'd had trouble when I was growing up in town?"

The girl nodded. "I'm so sorry. I'm just such a big blabbermouth."

"Don't worry about it. Everyone else knew. Why shouldn't your father?" And that explained the message on the mirror—probably meant to divert Hawk's investigation to some other suspect.

Tommy spoke up, more to Hawk than to Beth. "She was getting suspicious 'cause all the places that were hit had been her friends'. 'Cept Miss Haggerty. So we followed him out here last night. Guess he was checking up on the stuff. He'd been tellin' Annie Mae they were gonna move on soon. After he left..." The boy's narrow shoulders lifted in a shrug. "We came back at first light and that's when everything hit the fan. It all just caved in around us."

"You were lucky you weren't killed," Hawk said.

"Yeah. I know. We were sure scared. I mean, I had a flashlight 'n all, but geez...that place was like dark."

"Tommy was really brave," Annie Mae said in defense of her boyfriend. She squeezed the boy's hand where it rested on her shoulder. "He said someone would come. All we had to do was keep calm and wait." The girl said the words as though repeating a mantra she'd been rehearsing all day.

Help would have come sooner, Beth admonished herself, if she'd taken the time to be concerned about the young couple. Maybe if she'd acted more like Myrtle Symington, and blown the whistle sooner, the kids wouldn't have been trapped in a cave for nearly twelve hours.

The sun had already set, leaving a few traces of pink across the sky. The air had cooled considerably. Beth shivered.

Hawk took Beth by the arm and helped her to her feet. God, he was going to miss her. As she had talked with Annie Mae, it had struck hard in the gut that she had a lot of love to give. He wished he could claim just a piece of it, but that wasn't in the cards.

"Let's get these kids home," he said, his voice gravelly with emotion held in check. "Then I've got an arrest to make."

"Annie Mae's father?"

"Yeah." Hawk hoped Tommy's folks would let the girl stay at their house tonight. He didn't like the idea that she might witness her father's arrest. No kid should have to go through that. Hawk ought to know. More than once he'd seen his own father hauled off to the drunk tank. The memory brought the taste of bile to his throat. The worst kind of child abuse. He would have more easily dealt with a beating or two. Shame was a hard thing to overcome.

"What will happen to her?" Beth asked.

He shrugged. "Foster care, I guess. Till she's eighteen. I'll have to call the child welfare people at the county seat."

"But that's terrible, Hawk. She'll miss her senior year at high school."

"Not much I can do about it. Maybe somebody around here will volunteer to take her."

"I hope so. If I were going to..." Beth let the thought trail off. She wasn't going to stay in Newellton, and could hardly offer to share her tiny New York apartment with Annie Mae. There was so little space, they'd either have to get bunk beds or sleep in shifts.

Discouraged that she couldn't help Annie Mae, Beth jumped the first ribbon of water and landed awkwardly on the sandbar. Hawk steadied her with his hand at her elbow.

With an ache that was as much physical as emotional, Beth realized this could well be the last time Hawk ever touched her. He must have been aware of the same possibility because his hand lingered there for several beats longer than necessary.

"Guess you're all set to fly back to New York tomorrow," he said. They stood poised between two divergent parts of the river, just as their lives were about to take them along different routes into the future, a future where they would never come together again.

"I've got some more packing to do tonight. The real estate lady said she'd ship some things for me." The words came hard to Beth. To speak of ordinary things, arrangements that had already been made, was nearly impossible. Yet that's what she had to do. The other choice would be to say goodbye. That word would surely stick in her throat.

"You need a ride to the airport, or anything?"

"No. I'm okay." She wasn't okay at all. Bit by bit she was dying inside.

"Well, call if there's anything..."

"Thanks."

Hawk's shadowed gaze settled on her lips, and his hand drifted toward her face, just brushing against her work-tumbled hair. For a moment Beth thought he might kiss her, even though there were still dozens of people lining the river bank, and the last of the rescue workers were trudging past them. Instead his hand dropped to his side.

"Have a good flight."

Beth expelled the breath she'd been holding and the pain constricted her chest. *Goodbye, my love.*

Chapter Eleven

"**Y**ou mean to tell me you're satisfied to stay in this hole-in-the-wall office for the rest of your life?" Rick Ramsey sat in Hawk's chair behind a battle-marred desk. The chair squeaked when he tipped it back.

"I mean, I haven't reached a decision yet about running for sheriff. You'll have to give me a little more time." At the moment all Hawk could think about was Beth getting on that damn plane. Six hours to flight time. At the last check of his watch it had been six hours and five minutes. The whole situation had him feeling like the executioner's ax was about to fall and he was helpless to prevent the inevitable. She was so damn stubborn!

"What's the problem, son?"

Hawk paced across the room to the window and stared out onto Main Street. How did a guy answer a question like that?

The chair complained as Ramsey stood. "I see. Must be woman trouble."

"Good guess," Hawk admitted, his lips twisting into a wry smile.

"You talk. I'll listen."

Adjusting the angle of the dusty venetian blinds, Hawk said, "I was going to propose the other night. I didn't quite get around to it." Though the word marriage had been mentioned, for all the good it had done him.

"You were going to propose because *I* suggested it?"

"No, sir." Hawk turned. "Not on your life. I'd had it on my mind since the first moment I heard Beth was back in town." Maybe he'd always secretly hoped she would show up in his life again.

"Then why didn't you pop the question?"

"We had a little disagreement."

"So apologize. That's what we gotta do sometimes."

"I don't think it would be that easy."

"Do you love her?"

"Yeah." He looked away from Ramsey because a man was supposed to be stoic. And he didn't want his boss to see just how difficult that admission had been.

"She love you?"

"I thought so." Restlessness drove Hawk back across the room where he checked the lock on the weapons case. "She says I'm stodgy."

Ramsey's roaring laughter reverberated around the small office.

Hawk winced and scowled.

Finally controlling himself, Ramsey said, "Sounds like she's got you pegged." He wiped a tear from the corner of his eye with the back of his hand.

"Thanks a lot," Hawk grumbled under his breath. "She also doesn't want to live in Newellton. Ever. Things didn't go well for her when she was growing up around here, and she can't stand the thought of settling in the town."

"Then it sounds to me like you got a couple of choices, bucko. You can tell the lady adios, and stick around Newellton for the rest of your life. Or you can get your butt in gear and go find someplace where you could both be happy."

The furrows across Hawk's forehead tightened. "Then I'd really have to give up the thought of running for sheriff."

Ramsey looped his arm around Hawk's shoulder. "Let me tell you somethin', young man. There's nothin', absolutely nothin' in this world as important as the woman you love. I'm going to lose my Harriet. She's got cancer and...dammit all..." Tears pooled in the sheriff's eyes. "I'd give my soul for that woman. Whatever time we have left together, we're gonna enjoy. That's why I'm retiring."

"I'm sorry, Rick. I didn't know."

"Nobody does. And don't you go spreading the word. It's just that..." Ramsey's voice quavered. "If I had to choose between being county sheriff, or even being president of the good ol' U.S. of A., and having Harriet with me...well, it wouldn't take me two seconds to decide. Maybe you ought to think about that, son."

Hawk did. In between phone calls to the county seat to arrange foster care for Annie Mae, he thought about Beth. And checked his watch. Often.

Dammit all! He loved the woman. Sure he was conservative. Yeah, he admitted, *stodgy*. And that's exactly why he needed her. She was so bright, so much fun, she lit up his life as no one else could. While railing out at Beth about her impulsiveness, that's exactly why he loved her. She fought back, sometimes rightfully thumbing her nose at society. She was his opposite, his other half, the part of him he'd suppressed over the years in order to survive in a world that hadn't always been friendly.

So why did he think Newellton was so damn special? he wondered. His ancestors had roamed for centuries across thousands of square miles of open prairie. One particular spot wasn't all that important. With little effort, he could literally pick up his tepee and move on. Not that he wanted to try New York again. But maybe, just maybe, Beth would consider a compromise.

He sure as hell was going to give it one last try. Granted, seduction hadn't worked. *Or* being stodgy.

Darn it all, he thought, setting his jaw at a determined angle. He'd give Beth a little of her own medicine. She wasn't the only one who could be impulsive.

"Watch your mouth, Charlie."

Ignoring the bird, Beth eyed the curious gathering of townspeople in Grandma Claire's living room— Millie, Taylor Franklin, Irene Whitefeather and two other members of the rehab center board of directors. With only a few hours until her flight, it was a heck of a time for a social call.

"We had us a little meeting last night," Franklin said, acting as spokesman. He stood in the middle of the room, his thumbs slipping up and down behind his suspenders.

"If you hadn't called that nice young sheriff," Millie interrupted, "I just don't know what would have happened to my grandson. Such a dear boy."

A twinge of yesterday's guilt nudged Beth again. "I just wish I'd said something earlier."

"All's well that end's well, my Arnold used to—"

"Millie, will you stop talkin' long enough so I can get down to business," Franklin insisted.

"Of course, Taylor, dear. We're all eager for Beth to hear our idea."

Puzzled, Beth wondered if they'd decided a strip joint would be a good investment, after all. She glanced at Irene, who was sitting quietly on the sheet-covered couch. When their eyes met, Irene shrugged and a little smile twitched at the corners of her lips.

Franklin cleared his throat. "As we see it, this county has got no more 'n no less problems than any other county in the state."

"Man overboard!" Charlie hopped onto a lamp shade and peered out the front window.

Scowling, the mayor continued, "And our alcoholism rehab center is about the best there is. 'Course, we always need more money for extra programs and such. Irene, here, had this idea."

"Maybe I could explain what we have in mind," Irene suggested.

Franklin's mouth worked soundlessly for a moment, as though he wasn't quite ready to give up the floor. "Oh, go ahead," he finally conceded.

Beth felt like she was watching a tennis match as her attention shifted from the mayor to Irene.

"Art can be very therapeutic for recovering alcoholics," Irene explained. "They can express some of the pain they've experienced, and it keeps both their hands and minds occupied. At this point we have equipment and supplies, but no one to teach the residents the basics."

"We don't have much of a budget, either," Franklin pointed out.

Millie leveled the mayor a scolding look over the top of her glasses. "Pshaw, Taylor. You've been a pessimist since you were just a boy. Your mama used to fret about you. Worried you'd never amount to a hill 'o beans, and you finally did. We'll find the money."

Color rose on Franklin's cheeks.

"What we'd like to do," Irene continued calmly, "is hire a part-time teacher to hold regular classes two or three times a week."

"You're not thinking about me, are you?" Beth asked. She felt like she'd missed some very important part of the conversation. Things simply weren't making sense. Charlie seemed to know more about what was going on than she did.

"Of course that's what we have in mind, dear," Millie insisted, as though it were common knowledge.

"But my plane leaves in about five hours. My bags are packed. Everything's arranged." Beth was leaving Newellton, the one place on earth where she'd never felt welcome.

"It seems there's been some talk around town," the mayor said.

Beth rolled her eyes and clinched her teeth. More talk about a Haggerty girl?

"There was the dance the other night. And then you finding the lost youngsters. My wife says..." Franklin glanced uncomfortably around the room at the other occupants. They all gave him a nod of approval. "My wife says we lose our finest young people to the big cities. She thinks if we had more young folks around like you..."

He puffed out his jowls and Beth realized just how much this speech was costing Franklin. It was as close to an apology for the way he'd treated her as she could ever expect to receive.

"Folks with energy and creativity... those are her words... then maybe the kids wouldn't feel so stuck out in the middle of nowhere. They'd stay and help build up this town. Maybe make it an even better place to live."

"Mr. Franklin, are you actually asking me to stay in Newellton?" A possibility Beth had never considered.

He didn't meet her gaze. Perhaps that was too much to ask. "Yes, I guess I am," he muttered.

One of the board members, a lanky, narrow-faced man, spoke up. "We all think you'd be an asset to our organization."

Surprise and a keen sense of pleasure swept over Beth. She'd never thought in a thousand years anyone would actually *ask* her to stay in her hometown, much less offer a job. Of course, it didn't sound like the position would pay enough to support herself, unless...

"I think there's also a man in town who'd very much like you to stay," Irene said in a confidential tone.

Beth's head whipped around to look at her. She swallowed hard. "I'm not sure that's true."

"I saw him at dawn singing his morning prayers. He never does that, Beth. If something has come between the two of you, I think it's hurting him a great deal."

Beth was hurting, too. So much so there were times when simply drawing a breath was painful. "I don't fit in with what he wants." Maybe she'd gain marginal acceptance from Franklin, and people like Myrtle Symington. Perhaps the voters could accept the wife of the county sheriff as a bit impulsive. But those weren't the only issues Hawk would consider. "I mean...what would his tribe think if he married a blonde like me?" A person who was just this side of flamboyant.

Irene's lips quirked. "I think they'd like the way you keep his head on straight for him. Like calling him Big-Chief-Toma-Hawk. Most of us on the tribal council don't take ourselves quite as seriously as he does, and Hawk needs to lighten up a little. You'd be good for him."

Beth wasn't so sure. The last thing she wanted was to be an embarrassment to Hawk.

Promising Franklin and the others she'd give their proposal serious thought, even after she returned to New York, she escorted her guests to the door.

"S'long, toots!" Charlie called his final salute over Millie's shoulder.

Beth smiled. In just two weeks she'd grown incredibly fond of Millie Russell and that stupid bird. In an equally short time, she'd also identified a real kinship with Irene. She cared for Annie Mae, too, and wished she could do something to help the girl. In all the years she'd lived in New York she'd never had the same sense of belonging as she'd felt in the last half hour.

Small towns, she mused, offered opportunities that were quite different than the big city. There wasn't an art gallery for a hundred miles, much less a museum or professional concert hall. But there were people here who she could care about.

She let the screen door close behind her, thinking friendships were something special, wherever they might occur.

Admittedly she wasn't sure she'd ever be right for Hawk. At least, not from his perspective. But it was nice to feel like she belonged . . . as though she could settle roots into the land she'd always loved, too. You didn't have to be an Indian to sense a oneness with the big skies of Montana.

But could she stay in Newellton if Hawk didn't want her? she wondered. Her heart ached at the thought.

The part-time job with the rehab center would keep her in food. And, of course, she now owned Grandma Claire's house outright, with only minimal property taxes to pay, plus upkeep.

She did a quick mental calculation. It might just work out. Particularly if she could supplement her income by illustrating children's books. She wouldn't get rich but she could survive. Barely. And she'd have time to explore some of her untapped talents, those she had inherited from Jason Ambrose.

Not a bad plan. Like a hefty savings account, her ace in the hole would always be Grandma Claire's portrait. For now she'd like nothing better than to have the picture hanging over the fireplace mantel where she could gain inspiration from both the subject and the artist.

After making a few hasty phone calls to New York, Beth decided she'd have to talk to Hawk. Even if he didn't want her, she rationalized, he had a right to know about her plans.

Grabbing a sweater, she hurried out the door and down the steps, only to collide with a—

A horse? An Indian pony in Grandma Claire's front yard?

Her head snapped up. Her heart lodged in her throat.

Hawk towered above her. Mounted bareback, he wore only tight-fitting faded jeans and a grin so sexy it took her breath away. His hair hung loose across his bare shoulders; his broad chest looked so inviting her palms itched to touch him. He appeared primitive, very much like she had once sketched him, and thoroughly enticing. She felt a big chunk of herself melting at the heated look he gave her.

"What are you—"

In a startlingly fluid motion, he lifted her so she straddled the horse, her back firmly pressed against his hard chest, her hips nudging his groin. "I'm kidnapping you."

"You can't do that," she protested, an urge to giggle warring with an erotic sensation in her middle where Hawk's muscular arm circled her waist. "You don't even have any war paint on."

"I was in a rush. As it was, I had to borrow a horse from Irene's corral."

"You're a horse thief?" She nearly choked on the laughter that threatened.

"He belongs to Nick and I didn't have time to even leave a note. I was afraid you'd take off before I got here."

"I'd already called about the flight." To cancel my ticket.

"Forget your plane. You're not going back to New York." He reared the horse and wheeled him around to gallop down the street.

She grasped his arm. "But Hawk—"

"Women who are being kidnapped aren't supposed to argue."

"Of course they are." She loved what he was doing, the feel of her thighs resting against his and the whipping strands of their hair tangling together like lovers entwined. "Have you thought about what people will think?"

With incredible timing, Millie Russell chose that moment to come outside. She waved and called out, "Have a nice ride, children."

Beth groaned. More grist for the gossip mill.

"It doesn't matter what people think." He turned onto a street that circled the downtown area. Even so, a wide-eyed paperboy nearly fell off his bike at the sight of a horse and two riders bearing down on him.

"Have you been nipping on locoweed?" She felt giddy, intoxicated, completely in love. Hawk hadn't given up on her. "How can you expect people to vote for you for county sheriff if they see you doing a crazy stunt like this?"

"Who cares? I want everybody to know you're my woman. As for county sheriff, anybody who wants it can have that job, as far as I'm concerned. You're the most important thing in the world to me, Beth. We'll live any place you say. We'll make it work." His breath came hard and hot against her ear. "But right now, I'm taking you to my tepee. According to you white-eyes, ravishing a woman is an old Indian tradition."

A car coming from a side street braked hard, and the driver gawked at them through his windshield.

Beth nestled herself more deeply in his embrace, her heart so full of happiness she thought surely it would burst. She boldly rested her hand on his thigh, feeling the heat of his flesh through the denim fabric and memorizing the sensation. "Getting ravished by you sounds like a wonderful idea. After that we can start working on your campaign strategy."

"What?" He slowed the horse as they reached the far side of town.

Beth drew a shaky breath. Being kidnapped was downright exhilarating. She was sorry she hadn't suggested the idea herself. "I've got some great ideas for posters. How 'bout a picture of you smoking a peace pipe and the words Vote for Hawk, He Keeps the Peace?"

"Haven't you been listening? We aren't going to stay in Newellton."

"Gee, that's too bad because I've already decided this is a great place to live." And raise a couple of brown-eyed kids with wicked grins and hearts as big as the whole outdoors.

Hawk sputtered. "What the hell are you talking about?"

"That's what I was coming to tell you when you so *rudely* decided to kidnap me. I'm not going back to New York. I'm going to stay right here." Forever, she hoped, with the man she loved.

"Beth, have I missed something?"

"Yep." Grinning, she turned so she could look up at him. "You didn't have to kidnap me at all."

His eyes darkened. "You mean I've made a fool of myself for nothing?"

"Not exactly. It will be a great story to tell our grandchildren." She cocked her head. "I assume you're going to make an honest woman of me—after you have your way with me, of course."

"Right, Little-Brave-with-Big-Stick. That's the whole idea. Ring included."

"Good," she agreed smugly, delighted to learn he'd been so confident of her acceptance. "As long as you understand I can't change who I am, and I'm always likely to be a bit impulsive, I accept your proposal."

"You're perfect, Beth. Just the way you are." Blowing out a sigh of relief, Hawk said, "Now that that's settled, I have a confession to make."

She arched her eyebrows. "Oh-oh."

"I always felt like you, well, needed my protection. From guys who harassed you in parking lots and people like Franklin. I was wrong. You can hold your own just fine, without any interference from me."

"I'll always want you at my side, Hawk," she whispered, fighting against the happy tears that pooled in her eyes. "There is, of course, something else you ought to know, too."

He groaned. "I'm afraid to ask."

Giggling, she said, "I can't bear the thought of Annie Mae having to move away from her friends in her senior year. I want to be her foster mother."

"What do you know about being a mother?"

"Well, maybe *sister* is a better word. Still..." She ran her fingers through Hawk's long, silky hair. How free it made him seem, at one with the earth. She hoped he'd never cut it. "You could fix it, couldn't you? I mean with the child welfare people?"

Taking her hand, he let his thumb slide up and down the sensitive flesh of her inner wrist, sending tingling sensations to her heart. "It would be a little crowded for three in the tepee."

She swallowed hard. "There's plenty of room at Grandma Claire's house. Till your place is finished."

"*Our* place," he said, his voice filled with husky undertones.

They'd arrived at his tepee, and he slid off the horse, gently lifting Beth down to the ground next to him. He pulled her hard against the evidence of his desire.

"You are probably the most unpredictable woman in the entire world."

"You're not doing so bad yourself, Chief." She'd never expected Hawk to sweep her off her feet. And that's exactly what he'd done. With considerable class, she thought with a self-satisfied smile.

He nuzzled his lips against the column of her neck. "There's no way I'll ever be able to keep up with you."

Shivering, though she didn't feel in the least cold, she looped her arms around his shoulders, aware of the texture of his flesh as she kneaded his back, his heady, masculine scent and his strength. "I love you, Raymond Hawk. I always have."

He lifted her easily in his arms and carried her into the tepee.

"Welcome home, Beth," he whispered, lowering her in the muted light to his soft bed of fur pelts.

Epilogue

One year later

At the sound of Hawk's car in the driveway, Beth smiled and set aside her paintbrush. For once he was home early. No one had bothered to mention during the election campaign this past year that a county sheriff worked very long hours. She still remembered every precinct she'd walked and then the victory celebration. What a night that had been!

Awkwardly she got to her feet. The light was fading anyway outside the big picture window of her studio room, misting the expansive view she'd been painting. She'd been experimenting with acrylics, and it was going well. She even had a potential customer interested.

"How's it going, sweetheart?" Hawk asked, tossing his Stetson aside. He kissed her gently and placed his hand on her protruding stomach.

"Hmm. I think Little Beaver has acquired a horse. He's been galloping around inside there all day."

His lips twitched into a proud fatherly grin. "Probably practicing so he can kidnap his lady love."

"It worked for you."

"And I'd do it all over again in a minute."

Wrapping her arms around his waist, Beth leaned her head against his chest. His white shirt still felt crisp even at the end of the day. "You're home early."

"I had a meeting with Newellton's city fathers. Managed to convince them the expense of having two deputies instead of just one would be well worth it."

"Good for you."

"Where's Annie Mae?"

"She and Tommy are figuring out their next semester's class schedule at the community college. She'll be home for dinner."

"Ah." He nuzzled his lips at the sensitive spot beneath her ear with the intimacy of a lover who knew just how to arouse her. "Alone at last," he sighed.

She giggled. "With this big lump in my belly? We're definitely a threesome."

The phone rang and Hawk groaned. "If it's for me, tell 'em I'm out."

Smiling, and knowing she was the luckiest woman in the world, Beth picked up the instrument. Before she answered, she gave a quick wink at Grandma Claire's portrait in its place of honor over the fireplace. "Hawk residence."

"Beth? Beth Haggerty?"

She went very still, her hand gripping the telephone so tightly her knuckles ached. Her heart skipped a beat and then began to flutter wildly. The voice was so familiar....

"Marilee?" she whispered past the tightness in her throat.

"Yes, Beth, it's me. Your prodigal sister."

*   *   *   *   *

HE'S MORE THAN A MAN, HE'S ONE OF OUR

DADDY'S ANGEL
Annette Broadrick

With a ranch and a houseful of kids to care for, single father Bret Bishop had enough on his mind. He didn't have time to ponder the miracle that brought lovely Noelle St. Nichols into his family's life. And Noelle certainly didn't have time to fall in love with Brett. She'd been granted two weeks on earth to help Brett remember the magic of the season. It should have been easy for an angel like Noelle. But the handsome rancher made Noelle feel all too much like a woman....

Share the holidays with Bret and his family in Annette Broadrick's *Daddy's Angel,* available in December.

Fall in love with our **Fabulous Fathers!**

FF1293

Take 4 bestselling love stories FREE

Plus get a FREE surprise gift!

UNDER THE MISTLETOE

Where's the best place to find love this holiday season? UNDER THE MISTLETOE, *of course! In this special collection, some of your favorite authors celebrate the joy of the season and the thrill of romance.*

Available in December from

Silhouette

ROMANCE™

SRXMAS

The miracle of love is waiting to be discovered in Duncan, Oklahoma! Arlene James takes you there in her trilogy, THIS SIDE OF HEAVEN. Look for Book Three in November:

A WIFE WORTH WAITING FOR

Bolton Charles was too close for comfort. Clarice Revere was certainly grateful for the friendship he shared with her son. And she couldn't deny the man was attractive. But Clarice wasn't ready to trade her newfound freedom for love. Not yet. Maybe never. Bolton's patience was as limitless as his love—but could any man wait forever?

Available in November,
only from

Silhouette
R O M A N C E™

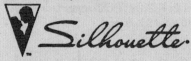

He staked his claim...

HONOR BOUND

by
New York Times
Bestselling Author

previously published under the pseudonym Erin St. Claire

As Aislinn Andrews opened her mouth to scream, a hard
hand clamped over her face and she found herself face-
to-face with Lucas Greywolf, a lean, lethal-looking
Navajo and escaped convict who swore he wouldn't hurt
her— *if* she helped him.

Look for HONOR BOUND at your favorite
retail outlet this January.

Only from...

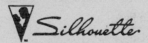

where passion lives. SBHB

Silhouette Books
is proud to present
our best authors,
their best books...
and the best in
your reading pleasure!

Throughout 1993, look for exciting
books by these top names in
contemporary romance:

DIANA PALMER—
The Australian in October

FERN MICHAELS—
Sea Gypsy in October

ELIZABETH LOWELL—
Chain Lightning in November

CATHERINE COULTER—
The Aristocrat in December

JOAN HOHL—
Texas Gold in December

LINDA HOWARD—
Tears of the Renegade in January '94

When it comes to passion,
we wrote the book.

BOBT3

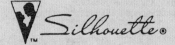

SILHOUETTE.... Where Passion Lives

Don't miss these Silhouette favorites by some of our most popular authors!
And now, you can receive a discount by ordering two or more titles!

Silhouette Desire®

#05751	THE MAN WITH THE MIDNIGHT EYES BJ James	$2.89	❏
#05763	THE COWBOY Cait London	$2.89	❏
#05774	TENNESSEE WALTZ Jackie Merritt	$2.89	❏
#05779	THE RANCHER AND THE RUNAWAY BRIDE Joan Johnston	$2.89	❏

Silhouette Intimate Moments®

#07417	WOLF AND THE ANGEL Kathleen Creighton	$3.29	❏
#07480	DIAMOND WILLOW Kathleen Eagle	$3.39	❏
#07486	MEMORIES OF LAURA Marilyn Pappano	$3.39	❏
#07493	QUINN EISLEY'S WAR Patricia Gardner Evans	$3.39	❏

Silhouette Shadows®

#27003	STRANGER IN THE MIST Lee Karr	$3.50	❏
#27007	FLASHBACK Terri Herrington	$3.50	❏
#27009	BREAK THE NIGHT Anne Stuart	$3.50	❏
#27012	DARK ENCHANTMENT Jane Toombs	$3.50	❏

Silhouette Special Edition®

#09754	THERE AND NOW Linda Lael Miller	$3.39	❏
#09770	FATHER: UNKNOWN Andrea Edwards	$3.39	❏
#09791	THE CAT THAT LIVED ON PARK AVENUE Tracy Sinclair	$3.39	❏
#09811	HE'S THE RICH BOY Lisa Jackson	$3.39	❏

Silhouette Romance®

#08893	LETTERS FROM HOME Toni Collins	$2.69	❏
#08915	NEW YEAR'S BABY Stella Bagwell	$2.69	❏
#08927	THE PURSUIT OF HAPPINESS Anne Peters	$2.69	❏
#08952	INSTANT FATHER Lucy Gordon	$2.75	❏

	AMOUNT	$ _____
DEDUCT:	10% DISCOUNT FOR 2+ BOOKS	$ _____
	POSTAGE & HANDLING	$ _____
	($1.00 for one book, 50¢ for each additional)	
	APPLICABLE TAXES*	$ _____
	TOTAL PAYABLE	$ _____
	(check or money order—please do not send cash)	

To order, complete this form and send it, along with a check or money order for the total above, payable to Silhouette Books, to: *In the U.S.*: 3010 Walden Avenue, P.O. Box 9077, Buffalo, NY 14269-9077; *In Canada*: P.O. Box 636, Fort Erie, Ontario, L2A 5X3.

Name: _____

Address: _____ City: _____

State/Prov.: _____ Zip/Postal Code: _____

*New York residents remit applicable sales taxes.
Canadian residents remit applicable GST and provincial taxes.

SBACK-OD

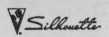